LONDON SPIES
By
SJ SLAGLE

Copyright, 2017

* * *

* * *

Thank you for downloading my book! I am happy that you have made it part of your library.

Special thanks goes to my editors, Cheri Mills, Pam Kilrain and Lauren Suplizio.

Enjoy these titles from SJ Slagle:

Sherlock and Me Series
The Case of the Starry Night
The Case of the Feathered Snitch
The case of the Ghost Horse

Single Titles

The Reunion
London Spies

SJ Slagle also writes western romances as Jeanne Harrell.
Enjoy these books from Jeanne Harrell:

Rancher Series
Rancher's Girl
Whisperer
Always and Forever
Being Emma
The Darkest Hour
Just Before Dawn

Rancher's Christmas

Westerners Series
Riding the River
Stream Ran Dry
Lonesome Creek
Cool Water
Avila Beach Winery Series
The Winemaker's Dilemma
Winemaker's Son
Single Titles
Persuaded

These Nevada Boys
Courting Polly's Daddy
Never Let Me Go
Shoulda Been a Rancher
Since I Fell for You
That Nevada Girl

Write SJ Slagle at jeanneharrellauthor@gmail.com
http://www.jeanneharrell.com

* * *

Dedicated to my cousin, Milmae Floyd Gray, for her incredible wartime experience in World War II and her public service career. She is an inspiration to my entire family.

* * *

TABLE OF CONTENTS

* * *

CHAPTER 1
London, 1945

Phyllis Bowden picked her way carefully across the debris-strewn street. Walking wasn't for the faint of heart this morning, any morning really, and she knew it. Rain had been falling steadily for the past hour and puddles formed in the oddest places. She had traveled this way every day for nearly eight months and the sight of broken store mannequins laying on the sidewalk and street made her breakfast threaten to come up.

She stepped over a plastic arm dislocated at the elbow and a half-clothed torso next to it. Her black leather boot stepped gingerly between a soggy pile of ruined clothing, and a hairless head with frozen eyes staring back at her. Shifting slightly, Phyllis moved to a small, empty space on the wet sidewalk and accidentally dropped her purse by the smooth pink back of a mannequin no longer part of a once chic display. She picked up the purse, brushed off the dirt and debris it had collected, and continued her winding route to the corner. It was a gauntlet actually as shiny plastic legs, severed heads and naked bodies lay in the shadow of the bombed clothing store.

Walking another street to the American Embassy was not much better than this one. She'd tried a few different routes when she first arrived, but it didn't seem to matter; London was still experiencing the odd buzz bomb and more stores and restaurants had been hit in the West End than not. Oxford and Regent Streets had been hit hard during the Blitz with its after effects still evident. Selfridges and Bourne & Hollingsworth remained standing, but the John Lewis store had been gutted one night after a catastrophic fire caused by several incendiary and high explosive German bombs had dropped with pinpoint accuracy. Burning debris caused the famous area to be closed off in an attempt to bring the fires under control.

Fires were not as common these days, but the devastating effects of German bombing Phyllis saw on a daily basis was a constant reminder that, although the war was winding down, the historic city lay in ruins. She was filled with pride for the Londoners who somehow were able to pick themselves up and continue on in spite of all that had happened to them during this war. A war that clung like smoke on her clothes. No matter how many times she washed her blouses, skirts and dresses, the smell of war remained. It was in her mind when she woke up in the morning and in her sight as she picked her unsteady way across the cluttered sidewalk by the ruined store.

Relieved, Phyllis made it to the corner and turned to glance back at the destroyed mannequins in her wake. Her whole body shuddered with the thought they could have been human bodies. She straightened, tucked escaping tendrils of dark curly hair, slightly damp now, under her hat and proceeded to the American Embassy. There was much work waiting for her and she needed to get on with it. That's what everyone was trying to do these days—just get on with it. Get busy living or get busy dying and heaven knows there had been enough dying.

Phyllis walked up to the Embassy door, smoothed her rain-splattered trench coat and opened the steel fortified door to walk in proudly. Her welcome was unexpected, to say the least.

* * *

CHAPTER 2

What in the world? People scurried up and down the immense hallway as if they weren't sure where they were going. Rats caught in a maze never had the worried expressions Phyllis saw now. Inside guards with stiff uniforms tried to direct frightened men and women to various offices to move them out of the fray. Even from her stunned position at the door, she could see the flinches when guards came into contact with nervous shoulders, quivering backs. No one wanted contact.

She glanced up to the second floor to see much of the same—slamming doors, a blur of humanity trying to find some place to hide. From what?

And then she saw it…something she never, ever dreamed she would see since she had started working for the War Department as a civilian several years ago. Coming down the long staircase was a two-man Military Police escort on either side of the American Embassy's Military Attache, Lt. Col. Ronald Lawrence—Ronnie they called him—being escorted in handcuffs! out the side door, probably to a waiting car.

To go where? And why?

It was a still life picture before her at this moment in time. Everyone had stopped to stare at the tall man with the reddening face as he tried to maintain a confident posture under duress. He didn't fight the shiny handcuffs that kept his arms locked behind him. He merely smiled to one and all, perhaps hoping they wouldn't be as terrified as he had to be.

Ronnie? Being arrested? It was unthinkable that the man she knew, her boss' boss, could have committed such a serious offense to be arrested in the American Embassy before all the men and women he worked with on a daily basis. Ronnie had been at the Embassy only two years and she had found him to be a pleasant, congenial boss, stern when needed, but never a taskmaster. He commanded with more of a velvet glove and had the respect of everyone she knew.

The Military Police officers, in their crisp blue wool uniforms, took a subdued Lt. Col. Lawrence out a side door closing it firmly behind them. The second the door clicked shut, bedlam broke out again with Embassy staff scurrying around like scared mice. Small groups cluttered in corners, no doubt gossiping about what they had just witnessed. Looking past the staircase, Lorraine Watkins caught her eye pointing toward a small office down the next hallway. Phyllis hurried after her and caught her trench coat in the door when she tried to shut it too quickly. Jerking on the material, she nearly tore part of the slick lining.

"What's going on, Lorraine? I just walked in the door and..."

"Where have you been, Phyl? You're late this morning."

"Well, you know how hard it is to walk past The Emporium. Those mannequins are still all over the..."

"Phyllis." Lorraine grabbed her arm to tow her to the nearest chair. She shoved her into it. "Sit and listen to me."

"All right, all right." Phyllis began to unbutton her coat. "Could I at least take my coat off?"

Lorraine shrugged. Phyllis watched her friend glance in a small mirror by the desk to pat her long pageboy hairdo with an upswept front curl. When she freshened her red lipstick, Phyllis laughed.

"So you rushed me in here to make sure you look good?"

"Hardly." Lorraine's worried eyes met hers. "You won't want to hear this."

"Then don't tell me."

She took a deep breath. "Lt. Col. Lawrence, our Ronnie, was arrested for espionage."

Phyllis blinked, utterly astonished at the news. "That can't be."

Lorraine nodded. "It is and now your boss, Dickie, is in."

That took a minute to sink in. Major Richard Simpson—Dickie they called him—was the new Military Attache? Phyllis had worked for the man for the eight months she had been assigned to the American Embassy, but had never warmed to him. He seemed like a good sort of man but she was never sure of her footing. He was mad one minute, then obsequious the next. Hot and cold, black and white, nervous and confident…she could never get a bead on what made him tick. She'd finally given up and was ready to ask for a transfer since whatever she did was never quite good enough. And now this.

"Dickie is the new Military Attache? I can't believe the President would want him in the job. He's too inexperienced, for one thing. Why not just appoint someone else like they did when Ronnie took the job from Col. Bradley?"

"I haven't the foggiest, but the word is you're going to be in the hot seat now."

"Why? What do you mean?"

"Didn't Dickie work closely with Lawrence?"

"Not that closely. Dickie doesn't confide in me, but every time they had a meeting, neither one looked happy coming out of it."

That stopped Lorraine for a moment. She bit her lip. "Maybe they didn't get much in the way of happy news."

Phyllis chuckled. "Astute comment, Lorraine. This is wartime. Besides," she slid her arms out of the trench coat, "Amy would have mentioned if there had been some kind of fight. She's been good that way."

Lorraine sat down on the chair behind her desk, picked up a file, glanced at it and threw in a pile by her typewriter. "Didn't know you and Amy were such good buddies."

"Don't pout," Phyllis kidded. She stood, headed for the door. "You're still my best friend, okay?"

"Well, okay." A slow smile spread across Lorraine's pretty face. "We still on for tonight?"

"After all that's happened today, probably every staffer in the Embassy will be at the corner pub."

"Then let's head to Blue Anchor. Hardy anyone goes there anymore after…"

"…It was bombed and never reopened?" she finished.

"No, silly. It's open, you just have to know the password to get in."

Phyllis laughed, opened the door. "Let's just meet at Angel's. It's small, quiet and hasn't been bombed—yet."

"After work?"

"Make it seven. I'll probably put in a long one today."

* * *

CHAPTER 3

Down another long hallway, Phyllis walked into a large room with plain beige walls and a high ceiling. Brightly lit globes hung down to illuminate the area below. Phyllis tucked the trench coat over her arm as she put on a smile and walked past more than a dozen worn wooden desks with equally tired-looking women behind them. The glances and outright stares she received were met with the fake smile now plastered on her warming face.

Was everyone scared to death? Were they blaming her for something?

Many of these women she considered her friends, but there were no friendly expressions staring back at her as her heels clicked on the polished tile floor. It was the only sound she heard besides the roaring of her madly pounding heart. After what seemed like a century, she arrived at her desk outside the Assistant Military Attache's office. The door was closed with muted voices within, so she hung her coat on the side coatrack and sat down at her desk trying to look more confident than she felt. It took every ounce of nerve to keep from glaring back at the obvious stares, but she concentrated instead on tasks at hand.

Working hard for the better part of an hour on a letter Dickie had dictated to her yesterday, Phyllis happened to glance at a woman the next row over. To her surprise, she saw the worried face of Amy Broadbent looking back at her. What was Amy doing in the steno pool? With Amy's drawn countenance and frightened expression, Phyllis could only guess at the depth of the woman's despair. She had been Ronald Lawrence's secretary and her desk was by the Military Attache's office on the next floor. Obviously, someone higher up had stuck her here for the time being. Maybe they didn't know what to do with her.

Phyllis offered a small smile that was eagerly accepted. Amy smiled back, then quickly looked around her before burying her nose in the paperwork stacked on her desk.

Several minutes sped by as Phyllis checked and rechecked her newly typed letter for typos and spelling mistakes. She was proud of her reputation as the best speller and grammarian on the floor and strove to keep up her own high standards. As soon as she approved the letter, she reached for a mailing envelope when her buzzer buzzed.

"Phyllis? Could you come in here for a moment, please?"

She pushed a button to respond.

"Certainly, Major Simpson. Should I bring my steno pad?"

"Not this time."

Straightening a wrinkle in her long, pleated skirt, Phyllis went into Dickie's office.

"Shut the door."

"Yes, sir."

Phyllis watched in confusion as Major Simpson paced behind his desk. Back and forth he strode with short, measured steps as if he were marching to a silent tune. She observed him clinically for a few minutes, since he took no notice of her at all.

Dickie was in a state.

The jacket of his olive-colored wool uniform was thrown carelessly on a chair nearby. Deep wrinkles on his slacks indicated much sitting, probably fretting and his beige shirt looked like he'd slept in it. His thin tie had been hurriedly knotted. A slight scruff showed on his unshaven face and his pale hair hadn't been combed. Finally, his pacing slowed and he looked over at her.

"Sit down, Phyllis." When she didn't move, he added, "Please."

When she sat on a chair in front of his desk, he raked shaky fingers through his hair making it look more disheveled, if that were possible. He finally sat down and stared at her grimly.

15

"I supposed you've heard what's happened."

"I'd like to hear it from you, Major."

Dickie took a deep breath and words gushed out, colliding frantically with one another. "Lt. Col. Lawrence has been arrested for espionage which is a crock of crap..." He glanced at her sheepishly. "Sorry."

"That's fine."

"...But he didn't do it. He wouldn't do it! He's a man of honor and purpose and this job meant the world to him, so I just don't see how and why this happened." When he paused for breath, Phyllis spoke.

"What does it mean for you, sir?"

The perplexed look he gave her turned hard making her squirm under his scrutiny.

"It means, Miss Bowden, that you and I are moving up a floor."

Her jaw dropped. "You mean..."

"Yes. The President has asked me to take over for Lawrence." Shaking his head wearily must have let all the air out of his argument. He plopped on his chair with a slacked jaw, clouded eyes and many new wrinkles on his young face—resignation dripping from every pore. He had changed from wildly upset to utter exhaustion in the span of a few minutes and Phyllis watched it all. Was he confiding in her? That'd be a first.

"You'll be called in for questioning by the FBI as will I be. In fact, everyone in the Embassy will be questioned. The higher ups suspected a leak and apparently they thought it was Lt. Col. Lawrence."

"But..."

"No buts, Miss Bowden. We're going to continue doing our duty to our country and hope things are sorted out in time." His gaze locked with hers. "Do you have any questions?"

"Honestly? About a million but they can wait for right now. Are we moving today?"

He nodded and rose. "This minute, in fact. Pack what you need for now. I've got movers coming in an hour to get the rest of our things." Dick grabbed his jacket, slipping arms into sleeves. "It'll be a gauntlet to get out of here, but stiff upper lip, as the English say."

He walked toward the door.

"One question, Major Simpson, before we go. I have to know why Amy Broadbent is sitting out there."

Dick shrugged, attempted to smooth his wrinkled slacks. "I don't know. It wasn't my idea." He leaned in, speaking softly. "But the higher ups are suspicious of her because she was Ronald's secretary. I wouldn't befriend her, if I were you. She may not be with us long and you'll be tainted by the same brush in their eyes."

She swallowed hard before walking through the door he opened for her. All eyes discreetly turned to them and she could feel the questions pounding through telepathy. She'd be asking questions too if the situation were reversed.

Grabbing her purse and a few steno pads, Phyllis plucked her trench coat off the rack and followed Dickie down the long aisle separating the many desks in the pool. Eyes bored into her from all directions producing a dainty fear that crept down her spine like a daddy long legs. She had no answers for anyone, much less herself, but was at this moment, 'one of them'. It was a hard realization coming on the heels of knowing she'd suddenly lost the trust of women she had worked with for months. Good months. Solid work. Solid camaraderie too, she thought, but…perhaps not.

Everything comes at a price, does it not?

* * *

17

CHAPTER 4

Every step Phyllis took on the staircase brought her closer to the new office. She should have been excited, over the moon! It was a promotion, wasn't it? But dread wrapped itself around her heart like plastic and she was almost suffocating. What happens now to Lawrence?

Dickie reached the office of the Military Attache before she did and walked in. She noted Lt. Col. Ronald Lawrence's name stenciled on the frosted glass door before filing in behind Dickie. Two offices were adjoined with a side door separating her office from his. Pointing at her desk in this outer office, Dickie walked briskly through to the office just beyond, shutting the door firmly behind him. Now she was really alone. Separated from her co-workers in the steno pool and separated from her boss as well. Feeling low, Phyllis removed the cover from the typewriter and stared at it as if it were a living thing. It was a newer model than the one she'd been using and electric too. A Dictaphone sat to one side and a new intercom too. She set about learning her new equipment.

A few tiresome hours later with Dickie ensconced in his new office, Phyllis was ready to crawl out of her skin. She knew he'd been making calls, since both lines were lit up on her phone, but he hadn't asked her to do one blessed thing for him. She practically fell on Lorraine with gratitude when her door opened and the cute blonde bounced in.

"What are you looking so happy about?" she asked her.

"What are you so sour about?" Lorraine let her gaze roam the squeaky clean office to fall on the typewriter. "And you've got a new typewriter! Well, la de da…someone's coming up in the world."

"Unlikely it's me," scoffed Phyllis reaching in a drawer for her purse. "Let's get out of here for an hour and have lunch."

"You read my mind."

"Just a minute. Let me tell Dickie I'm going."

Lorraine's eyes widened. "He's still here?"

"Well, yeah, he..."

"Because lots of the higher ups are meeting in the conference room. Huh...wonder why he isn't there."

Phyllis wondered the same thing as she pushed the intercom button to his office.

"Major Simpson? I'm going to lunch."

"Sure, sure," came the quick reply. "I'll see you later."

"Will you be here?"

"Most likely."

Down another long hallway, they stuck heads in the Officers' Mess to see how many people were in there.

"Looks like the coast is clear."

"Oh, ha, Lorraine. I'm not afraid to eat here. Are you?"

She headed toward the buffet dishes on tables lined against a wall. "People have been snotty to me, probably guilt by association." Picking up a plate, she passed a heated dish of roasted potatoes and headed straight for the ham slices.

Phyllis picked up a plate and followed behind her. "Please tell me what I did to warrant being ostracized by everyone in the steno pool."

Lorraine forked a thin slice of ham unto her waiting plate. "Oh, I don't know. Maybe because you're fleeting up and they're not. You're calling attention to yourself and they don't like any secretary to be singled out." She loaded the rest of her plate with lettuce and tomatoes. "Look! That shipment of tomatoes finally got here and cheese from New Zealand. Heavenly!"

Phyllis glanced at the buffet dishes and sighed. "Can't tell you how much I miss fresh milk. I think I'd give up my monthly salary for a liter."

"I hear you."

Phyllis slowly put a small serving of salad on her plate. After dripping a tablespoon of dressing on the top, she made for a corner table. Lorraine took a slice of berry pie as well and followed her.

"That's all you're going to eat?"

"Not hungry, Lorraine."

"Sweetie, you need to eat more than that to keep up that peaches and cream complexion of yours."

Phyllis rolled her eyes as she stabbed a leaf of lettuce. "And quit trying to deflect the topic."

"What was the topic?"

"Why I'm being ostracized. I don't buy the 'fleeting up' answer."

Lorraine chewed a bite before swallowing and poured a glass of water from a pitcher on the table. "Want some?" Phyllis nodded. "Okay. Here's the scoop."

Phyllis scooted her chair closer to Lorraine and leaned in. "Tell me."

"Everyone is scared shitless."

"About me?"

"You're just collecting collateral crap being flung your way. Whenever there's a new Military Attache, people fear being shuffled around, being reassigned."

"But?"

"But this situation is different. Ronnie was arrested for espionage and everyone's ducking for cover. The career diplomats are scared out of their wits and so too are their secretaries. There's no safe haven for anyone right now, so expect some nasty looks for a while."

"I didn't cause this to happen. I like Ronnie."

She patted Phyllis' arm. "I know, sweetie, but your boss made it to the bigs and the atmosphere is suspicious of everything and everyone right now. At least until we all make it through questioning." Lorraine reached for the saltshaker.

"When does that start?"

"Rumor is that it already has. Minnie and Molly were called upstairs right before I came up to get you."

Phyllis froze with her fork heading towards her mouth. When she stopped to stare at her friend, a tomato fell back on her plate. "Minnie and Molly? What in the world could they know?"

Lorraine's shoulders moved up and down. "They work for the undersecretaries and probably know more than we do about statistics, numbers and plans."

"I don't know much, Lorraine."

She poked Phyllis with her fork.

"Hey!"

"Hon, we all know more than we say. We all take dictation and type reports and travel orders. We're all military intelligence and thus, our work is classified."

Other women began to file into the room. Several took one look at the occupants of the corner table and sat as far away as possible.

"Sure you want to be seen with me?" asked Phyllis. "We could be sharing national secrets."

Lorraine snorted. "They know better than to mess with me, but I'd watch myself if I were you. Don't head for any supply closets any time soon."

"I'm fine, Lorraine. That hasn't happened for six months or so."

"Still..."

"It's not a problem."

"If you say so."

After finishing their lunch, both women dumped their dishes into a bin towards the back. They tucked trays in a bin alongside and made their way towards the exit.

"I'm going to say hi to Martha. Her desk was next to mine in the steno pool."

Lorraine arched an eyebrow. "I wouldn't if I were you, but I'm not you...so go ahead."

Phyllis patted her curly bob, licked her lips and started towards the table of women. If looks could kill...*what did she do?*

"Hello Martha." She nodded at the other women. "How's your lunch today?"

A stout woman with an irritated expression looked up. "Fine." She turned her face away.

"Did you get those new typewriter ribbons you ordered? I know that must have..." Her words trailed off with the icy reception facing her. "Well, I'll leave you to your lunch."

No one at the table said another word and Martha looked angry that she'd bothered to speak to her.

Phyllis hurried out the door with Lorraine on her heels. "They're acting as if I was caught doing espionage with Mr. Lawrence. How can they think that?"

"Shh," Lorraine shushed her. "Don't even say something like that out loud. Don't think it. You think you have it bad—guilt by some kind of association—how do you think Amy feels? No one has spoken to her all morning."

"Dickie mentioned she might be transferred to another pool."

"...Or how about another embassy? This one isn't going to thaw out any time soon."

They walked quickly up the staircase towards Phyllis' office. "And what ever happened to 'we're all in this together'?"

"I guess all bets are off when one of us has been accused of being a spy."

At the office door, Phyllis hugged Lorraine. "Thanks for being my friend. It can't be easy for you. See you at Angel's later?"

"Seven, you said." She hugged her back.

"Quit wrinkling my new dress."

"Polyester doesn't wrinkle."

They laughed, lessening the tension. After Lorraine left, Phyllis opened the door with Major Richard Simpson now stenciled on the frosted glass, took a deep breath and peeked in cautiously. Dickie was still on the phone, so she worked on the new reports sitting in her inbox for the next few hours. With no one to talk to or gossip with by the water cooler, she finished her work more quickly than usual.

Wondering what to do next since Dickie still hadn't come out of his office, she went down the hall to get more carbon paper from the supply closet. When she got there, Phyllis realized she hadn't gotten a key for this new closet and was surprised to find the door ajar. She opened it tentatively sticking her head in for a look. Shelf after well-stocked shelf lured her in for an even closer examination. What riches! There were boxes of paper, spools of ribbons, tablets of lined paper and box after overflowing box of pens and pencils.

Her happy eyes widened at the bounty, her fingers itched to touch the treasure before her. Everyone was saying the war was nearly over, but that didn't mean she could get the supplies she needed in any sort of timely order. What the soldiers needed, of course, came first. She and every other secretary at the Embassy, on the first floor at least, were accustomed to shortages; it was just a part of life.

Reaching a hand for a beautiful fountain pen and a jar of black ink, the door suddenly slammed shut. Phyllis froze with her hand outstretched. Only a fraction of light from under the door reflected on the closet floor; she tried to step toward it, but her legs wouldn't move. Her breathing became short puffs, while perspiration beaded on her forehead. She could feel her heart beating faster just as nausea hit. A small stool caught her before she went down and Phyllis stuck her head between her knees. Passed out on the cold cement floor would not look dignified for the secretary of the Military Attache. Cupping her hands around her mouth and deep breathing stopped the hyperventilating, but hot flashes heated her sweaty skin.

Haltingly, she slunk to the door and tried the doorknob. Locked! From the outside? What the...

She pounded on the door until her fist hurt. No one came. She pounded more until the door seemed to sway with the incessant force. Just when she was about to keel over, someone opened the door. Phyllis fell straight into Dickie's arms.

"What the hell were you doing in the supply closet?"

"I was locked in, sir."

"How can that be?" He helped her to the office and sat her down.

She blew out a ragged breath, gazed off into space. "I'm sure I don't know, Major."

"I know we're newbies up here, but damn it, Phyllis. I need you to pull your weight. I'm close to sinking in the swamp and I can't save you too."

"I'm fine, sir," she puffed. "Just let me catch my breath."

He poured her a glass of water. "Here, drink this. I can't have my secretary falling apart on our first day." Dickie grabbed her shoulders looking her in the eyes. "I need you, Miss Bowden. Can I count on you?"

"Yes-s, sir, of course you can."

"Do you have a problem I don't know about?"

"I'm fine, sir." She straightened in the chair, handed him back the glass. "You can count on me."

"Damn straight. Now I've got to meet with a few people. Get your pad and meet me in the conference room in ten minutes."

"Okay."

After Simpson left, Phyllis wearily leaned back in her chair. She pulled a small compact from her purse to check her makeup before joining him. The woman in the reflection had flushed cheeks, watery eyes and lips devoid of color. The tube in her purse refreshed her lipstick and she wiped her eyes of excess moisture. While her cheeks calmed, Phyllis combed her curly hair. Spying a light hair amongst the dark, she plucked it out, smoothing her frightful brows. She dabbed powder on her smooth cheeks and turned this way and that to check the result of her work. Too bad the salon down the street had been bombed because she could use a manicure too.

When she felt she was presentable, Phyllis ran nervous fingers down the front of her dress, grabbed her pad and pencil and made her way to the conference room. Whatever she felt about the scene in the supply closet would have to wait. No terrible memories of that childhood trauma were going to overwhelm her now.

She had a job to do.

* * *

CHAPTER 5

Amy Broadbent opened a lower drawer to take out her purse. She was going home. At last! It had been a long, miserable day and all she wanted to do was soak in a hot tub. Maybe that would relax the concrete she felt in her shoulders after a day of being snubbed, ignored and, in general, shit upon.

And for what?

She had been the secretary to the Military Attache, Ronald Lawrence. Now the infamous Ronald Lawrence whose class, distinction and genuine duty to office and country seemed forever burnished in the eyes of everyone at the American Embassy. Her mind was occupied with unwelcome thoughts as she slid arms into her long coat and attached her hat with a colorful hatpin. She could at least look nice, even if she wasn't feeling very well at all.

Amy waited until all the other women in the steno pool had left the massive room. She glanced around at the ancient desks, typewriters poised at the ready. Pencils were sharpened for tomorrow's dictation and the room had been swept clean. Everything was in order and all was calm. But with her heart beating a mile a minute, she knew her life would never again know order, would never again know true calm. She felt deep in her gut that nothing would be the same.

Was there anything she could do about that?

Her shoulders continued to slouch although she made a real effort to straighten them. Even her good posture was failing her. And then she saw Phyllis Bowden come down the stairs. She'd obviously taken dictation at one of the super-secret meetings upstairs. Phyllis' shorthand skills were well known and she wasn't surprised to see

Phyllis stepping into her shoes so soon. Sometimes, that's the way it went in military intelligence…no one really trusted anyone else and no one talked about anything of importance. At least not in the hallways, Officers' Mess or steno pool. Seeing Phyllis gave her an idea.

"Phyllis?" Amy stepped out of a small alcove to make her presence known.

"Amy? You're still here?"

"Just leaving."

They stood together, saying little.

"I can't imagine what you must be thinking of me," she began.

Phyllis shook her head. "Don't even go there, Amy. My day has been one for the books too, although I'd rather forget than have it written down somewhere."

Amy chuckled. "Just because you took over for me shouldn't automatically make you suspicious."

"And just because you worked for Ronnie doesn't make you suspicious either."

"Thank you," she said quietly.

"Well, ah…I need to gather my things."

"Phyllis? Would you please have dinner with me tonight?"

"Um…"

"Because I feel if I can't talk to someone, I'm just going to explode."

Phyllis smiled, reached over to touch Amy's arm. "No exploding in the hallways. You know how maintenance hates that kind of cleanup."

"Do you…would you, please?"

Amy didn't know what was on her face, but a muscle in Phyllis' jaw contracted and for an instant she looked upset. She stepped away. "I don't mean to insult you or anything…"

Phyllis grabbed her arm. "No, it's fine. Let me get my coat and hat and I'll meet you by the front door."

"Sure you want to be seen with me?"

She laughed. "I can chance it. Only Lorraine would eat with me today, so being ostracized is going around. Wait for me."

* * *

CHAPTER 6

A strange yet familiar sight awaited them as they walked down the street away from the American Embassy. The route included large brick buildings, four and five stories high, with tarps waving in windows long ago blown out by German bombs. Statues of prominent British statesmen and royalty stood as silent witnesses to the devastation around them. While one side of the street still had standing buildings, shops and apartments, the other side had been completely obliterated during the Blitz. People had worked hard to sort out the mess the best they could, but wood fragments, bits of brick and broken concrete heaped in enormous mounds continued to decorate the site. A constant reminder they were still at war and death was only a heartbeat away.

Phyllis had applied for this position in the American Embassy in London from her cushy job at the War Department in Washington, D.C. because she wanted to make a difference for English civilians caught in a war between good and evil. She knew helping the war effort from war-weary England would make more of an immediate impact and that was important. She and Amy said little as they made their way through the devastation of the once beautiful city. The moment didn't call for small talk and the ruination only made them more conscious of the significant work they were doing. For the English, for the Americans, for every single person threatened by German domination.

It would be forever humbling.

Angel's stood out as the only small pub still in business in a block where most of the buildings had been mostly blown away. Fire had nearly destroyed the pub as well, but dedicated patrons had shown up before firemen to save what they could. Due to their brave efforts, the owner of the pub gave out free beer every Tuesday, which naturally collected a crowd. Luckily, this wasn't Tuesday but the bright green entrance with colorful flowers in front flowerboxes gave the appearance of all's well and 'we're happy to still be here'. Phyllis and Amy walked in the open doorway expecting a pleasant welcome, which is what they received. Mick, the owner, knew many of the Embassy employees and was proud to have their business.

"Ladies! Have a seat. I'll be right with you."

"Do you think it's stamped on our foreheads that we work up the street?"

Phyllis laughed. "I confess I'm in here more than I should be, so the blame lies with me."

They found a small corner table, took off their coats and hats and settled in.

"I haven't been in here before."

"Really, Amy? How come?"

"I had an English boyfriend for a while and he preferred pubs closer to his neighborhood in Notting Hill." She glanced around. "We never stopped in here, but I wish we had."

"Why's that?"

"Because," she grinned, "it looks like it probably did when Henry VIII was on the throne. Wood floors, plain wooden tables with chairs that don't match and a chimney I'd be scared to light."

"Don't forget the pictures of previous kings and queens decorating the unpainted walls and the ancient beer barrels holding up the bar."

They laughed and Amy picked up the one-page menu. Phyllis plucked it out of her hands.

"Don't bother. Mick only has one or two dishes on the menu and if you don't like what he has, don't order. Generally, he orders for us anyway."

Mick was heading across the room. A giant of a man, he had to duck under a low beam to lumber to their table.

"Ladies. What can I bring you to drink?"

Amy looked at Phyllis who whispered, "Let me handle this."

"We'll have two of the stout ale, Mick. Still got some?"

"Always, my fine ladies and how about supper? Tonight John's cookin' Cumberland Pie."

Phyllis blinked, surprised. "Cumberland Pie? You have beef?"

Mick blushed, stuck a large hand in his pocket. "Well…no. You know we ain't got no beef, Miss Phyllis, but…" he brightened before continuing, "my sister has a victory garden with lots of great vegetables and you know what a great cook old John is. Why he can make Toad in the Hole without sausage, but you could swear you was eatin' it all the same!"

"So we'll think we're eating Cumberland Pie with beef, but we won't be."

"Yes, ma'am!" Mick's smile showed a tooth missing in the front, yet his enthusiasm was infectious. His love of country had been proven time and time again, another reminder to Phyllis why she loved living here.

"Two, if you please." Phyllis held up two fingers.

Mick mimicked two fingers back. "V is for victory."

"And victory is at hand."

"God save the King!"

"God save the King, Mick."

He beamed and left to bring over two glasses of warm ale in short order.

"So you come here often?" asked Amy. Her first sip left a frothy layer on her upper lip. Phyllis pointed it out making Amy laugh.

"Thank you."

"For what?"

"Phyllis, I haven't laughed this much in ages. It's wonderful to not feel uneasy every second."

"May I ask what happened to the boyfriend?"

Her happy face drooped in an instant. Tears pooled in her eyes before sliding down her cheeks. Phyllis laid a hand on hers.

"Hey, I didn't mean to make you cry. He broke up with you?"

She took another drink, a hefty one this time, and wiped the froth from her mouth with a shaky hand. "He was...killed."

Phyllis' lips parted. "I'm so sorry. What happened?"

"He was a...gunner in the RAF and was shot down. He was listed as missing in action, but I'm assuming he's dead."

"What was his name?"

"Colin Hughes. We actually met at the Embassy—he came in with his commanding officer for a meeting and we took to each other immediately. After a cup of coffee in the cafeteria, he asked me out that night."

"How'd he manage to get away from his commanding officer?"

"Lt. Col. Lawrence wanted a private meeting and told us both to shoo for half an hour." Amy smiled at the memory. "Thirty minutes later, we were hooked." When her eyes flooded with tears again, Phyllis fished a tissue from her purse.

"All that's happened this week has hit you harder because he's gone."

"He was shot down only six months ago," she sniffled. "I know I'm still grieving, but I never expected to be ostracized as well."

Phyllis looked into the face of active suffering. "Maybe it would help to talk about it."

"Which? Colin's or my boss' demise?" She tucked the tissue in a pocket.

"Both."

"I miss Colin very much and I miss Ronnie too." She leaned toward Phyllis. "He didn't do what he's been accused of, Phyllis. I'm sure of it."

"Here you go, Miss Phyllis and friend! Two hot Cumberland pies fresh from the oven." Mick set two steaming plates before them. "Yeah, if I do say so myself, old John cooks the best pies from Knightsbridge to the West End. Been doing it most of his life, he has." His broad smile stretched across his moon-shaped face. "Eat hearty!"

32

Both Amy and Phyllis had been startled at Mick's boisterous announcement and physically shrank at his presence. Phyllis recovered first.

"Thanks so much, Mick. I'm sure this will be delicious."

They ate quietly for several bites before Phyllis ventured a word. She lowered her voice.

"How do you know that Ronnie didn't do anything, Amy? Do you have any proof?"

Amy put down her fork, wiped her mouth with a napkin. "I was with him every day for the two years he was Military Attaché. He let me in for every meeting, every conference and I listened to many of his phone calls."

"Why?"

"He wanted someone else on the phone with him…just in case."

"In case of…"

"In case of what happened today, I guess."

Phyllis took a sip. "Maybe he was meeting someone away from the Embassy, passing on information at a secret rendezvous."

"I highly doubt it. The man had a family here—his wife, Margaret, and three daughters. He never would have put them in jeopardy."

"Where's his family now?"

"I spoke with them this afternoon and they're going back to the States as soon as they get the okay from the FBI and the Army. I can't imagine the cloud they will be under in Washington until all this messy business is sorted out."

Phyllis fell quiet thinking about what Amy had said. As she chewed, she thought Amy's absolute confidence in Ronald Lawrence seemed genuine and she wondered, not for the first time today, just what was going on.

Amy picked at her food, pushed it around her plate.

"I'm sensing there's another question here."

"Phyllis, I need to ask you something." She pushed her plate to one side.

"I was right…"

But Amy didn't smile at her little joke; she was past laughing matters apparently.

"You're in a perfect position right now."

Phyllis waited for her to explain. When she didn't continue, Phyllis put down her fork. "Perfect position for what?"

Various emotions swept Amy's face. When she took a deep breath, her final expression was grim. "To find out what's going on at the Embassy. There's a rotten apple somewhere."

Too stunned to reply, Phyllis took a huge gulp of her beer. A quarter of the liquid drained from the glass before she set it down.

"Just hear me out."

Phyllis shook her head. "What can I do? I'm not in Investigations. I'm just a secretary."

"No one is just a secretary here. You may be writing reports or typing travel orders, but a secretary knows most of what her boss is doing. That's why I'm certain that Ronnie is innocent."

"How am I in a perfect position?"

"Because you're Dick Simpson's secretary. You will soon find out many things that the rest of us have no knowledge of. I speak from experience that your position in military intelligence just went up a notch in classified status."

Both hands curled around her warm glass. "Amy, what can I do?"

"Listen. Listen hard. Anything that doesn't seem right, probably isn't. Be curious of anything out of place. Watch Dickie like a hawk. He may know something; he may know nothing, but he's up there where the stream of intelligence is rapidly flowing. I know you have great ears, my friend, and if anyone can sort this out, you can."

"That's what the FBI is doing and maybe MI5."

"MI5? What's that?"

"British security service."

Shaking her head briskly, Amy leveled a cool look her way. "They've made a mistake. I'd stake everything I hold dear on it. In

34

fact…" she looked away, then locked her gaze on Phyllis. "I swear on Colin's grave that someone else is the spy, not Lt. Col. Lawrence."

"Amy…I just can't do it. I'm not a detective, I…"

"Don't tell me again you're just a secretary because I know how thoughtful you are, how inventive you've been when it comes to replacing the constant shortages."

Phyllis refrained from rolling her eyes. "One thing has nothing to do with the other."

"I know you have the skills to do this, if you really try. Ronnie once commented on your cleverness. Remember one week when our ration books hadn't arrived and you were able to locate enough food for our daily lunches?"

"Amy, that's…"

"And how about the time supplies went missing and you found out what happened to them?"

Phyllis coughed, shook her head.

"Please tell me you'll at least consider it. There's lives at stake, innocent lives. Ronald, his family, everyone at the Embassy is under suspicion—the heat won't be off until there's a guilty verdict or the real spy is discovered."

Amy stood, slipped on her coat. She looked through her purse. "Do you have any cigarettes because I don't." She laid some money on the table.

Phyllis waved her away. "Don't worry—I've got a few for the tip."

"I need to go. Tomorrow promises to be as horrible as today, so I'd better get some sleep."

"Wait, Amy…"

"I've said enough, probably too much." Her eyes beseeched Phyllis. "Think it over?"

"I doubt I'll think of anything else," she muttered.

The brief smile was there and gone. "Good. That's all I ask. See you tomorrow."

"Yeah. See you tomorrow."

Phyllis watched the small woman leave the pub with lingering sadness. She felt like melting into a pool on the floor. Instead she raised her glass to Mick who soon brought another stout ale to the table. Whatever he saw on her face, Mick set the glass down, collected Amy's dish and beat a hasty retreat behind the bar. The place had filled up during her conversation with Amy and she tipped her head towards a few regulars she'd seen from time to time. She studied the brown liquid in her glass.

You've got to find out what's going on.

There's a rotten apple somewhere.

A rotten apple.

She didn't think Ronald Lawrence was a bad man either. Certainly, he wasn't a spy. Or was he? If the Military Attache was in a position to leak intelligence, would Dickie soon take up the slack? What did Dickie honestly know?

He'd sounded genuine when he proclaimed his innocence this morning to her, but had that been an act? With the shock of the situation wearing off, Phyllis was thinking more clearly than she had all day. And what did she determine? That what Amy asked of her was impossible. She couldn't spy on her boss—it would be like spying on her own country.

Maybe 'spy' was too strong a word. It was certainly too strong to say out loud. That word brought the MPs, the FBI, and the condemnation of England, America and the Allied world. It was no small thing.

Sipping her ale, her vision blurred and Phyllis' mind wandered to yesterday at the Embassy. Dickie had been anxious. Her colleagues in the steno pool had been snippy, curt with one another. Everyone had been on edge or was she just imagining it now that she was looking back? She'd taken some papers upstairs to Lawrence's office and the expression on his face was inscrutable. No, she decided, reaching into her memory—his features were drawn and anxious too.

36

At the time, Phyllis had written all the anxiety off to the buzz bombs that had fallen the night before. They were horrible occurrences with such devastating consequences. Amy had commented that Lawrence's residence had narrowly avoided being bombed. But her face too held a certain reserve. Usually Amy was one of the cheeriest secretaries around, but not that day. Maybe Ronnie's anxiety had rubbed off on her, or maybe Phyllis was reading something more into the whole scene than actually happened.

She shook her head and was still mulling over Amy's request when Lorraine showed up later, scolding her for meeting some guy before she got there. Phyllis had told Lorraine a white lie to meet earlier with Amy. Keeping their meeting on the down low seemed a wise move and proved to be the smartest thing she'd done all day.

Yeah, Amy was talking nonsense.

* * *

CHAPTER 7

"Phyllis!" came the call from downstairs.

"What, Mrs. Stewart?" She walked to the top of the staircase and peered down at her diminutive landlady. She was no larger than a garden sprite, but could breathe fire at her or any of Phyllis' four roommates like a medieval dragon.

"Phone for you—again. It's that crabby sister of yours." Phyllis started down the stairs quickly. "Tell her to quit calling at such late hours. Supper was long ago and decent people are going to bed now."

"I will, Mrs. Stewart. I'm so sorry to inconvenience you."

"Again…"

"Yes, ma'am."

Phyllis hurried down to the main floor of the large row house where she and her roommates rented rooms while living in London. On a small table next to the library sat a large, black telephone used by everyone. She picked up the receiver, but waited until Mrs. Stewart went back into her flat before speaking into it.

"Hello?"

"I really think you should come home."

"Mary Ellen," Phyllis sighed. "Don't start this again."

"You're out wandering the world when your duty is here at home."

"I'm not wandering around the world. You know I'm stationed in London and I can't just up and quit my job. This is wartime!"

"Don't give me that I-have-a-duty-to-my-country stuff."

"It isn't *stuff*! I have a job to do."

"You're a civilian working as a stenographer in the American Embassy. You can come home any time you want."

Phyllis took a calming breath, then another. "I'm a civilian working in the Office of the Military Attache, located in the American Embassy in the personnel branch of the Military Intelligence division, if you want my exact job description, sis. And I signed a contract."

"I know, I know and with a G-2 clearance. Big deal."

"It *is* a big deal, Mary Ellen! It's a classified status as well. I shouldn't even be talking to you about this on the telephone."

Silence on the phone line stretched to a minute.

"Is that all you called about?"

"Dad's worse. With Mother gone and my family to care for, I've got my hands full. I need help, Phyllis, and I need you to come home."

Phyllis sighed. "Just because you're my older sister doesn't mean you can dictate my life to me."

"I'm trying to appeal to your sense of common decency." Her voice rose. "We're your family and you're letting us down!"

"Shh, Mary Ellen. Keep your voice down."

"Tell that nosy landlady of yours to keep her nose out of our business. Why, do you have any idea what she says to me when I call?"

Phyllis had a pretty good idea, since she always got a ration of complaints from Mrs. Stewart too.

"Phyllis?"

"Tell me what's going on with Dad."

"His doctor said the cancer has spread to his lungs. I don't know how long he will last—you *must* come home!"

"You know travel is restricted right now."

"They're saying here that the war is almost over."

"It'll be over when it's over, sis. I'm here for the duration; even hopping on a passenger ship now—if I could get a ticket—would still take four or five days to get there, depending on whether or not we go through any waters with active mines."

"How about military transport?"

"That's a no go right now too."

Mrs. Stewart stuck her head out the door. "You've been on long enough, Phyllis. Someone else, God forbid, may need to use the telephone."

"Of course, Mrs. Stewart."

Mary Ellen groaned. "What does that old bitty want now?"

"I have to go. I'll send more money next paycheck, so maybe you can hire someone to help you. That's going to have to do for now."

"And I haven't even gotten into why an attractive young woman like yourself isn't married yet."

Phyllis chuckled. "We can save that for next time."

"Take care, little sister. We miss you."

"I love you. Pass it on to the rest of the family."

"I will. Bye."

"Bye."

She carefully hung up the phone knowing that Mrs. Stewart was listening at the door. Phyllis hurried back upstairs and made it safely into her bedroom without encountering the tiny tyrant again. Whew…she closed the door quietly and walked over to stoke the dying embers in the fireplace. With little gas heat in the row house, she and her roommates were thrilled with individual fireplaces and tended them meticulously.

Watching the fire, Phyllis' thoughts strayed to Amy's words. Wild words. How could she even think that Phyllis would be able to act upon her request? Sure, she felt extreme pity about Mr. Lawrence, but stepping into another kind of fire was not Phyllis' definition of duty. But she did think of something else she could do that might shed some light on the turmoil and went to bed with a weary heart. The coming days were going to get rougher, she had no doubt, and not only because of the buzz bombs and this hideous war.

40

* * *

CHAPTER 8

It hadn't seemed possible that today could be worse than yesterday, but it sure was. Phyllis had had to travel up and down the stairs several times to give papers to someone in the steno pool and whenever she'd called, no one would pick up. After her fifth march to the steno pool, she was ready to bite someone's head off.

Dickie was no help. He was fighting his own battles. Stepping into Ronald Lawrence's shoes was turning out to be a bigger job than he had thought. His irritation and insecurities spilled over onto Phyllis who had nowhere to go with her own. She'd had no time for lunch and couldn't wait for the day to be over. With a rumbling stomach and imaginary knives sticking out of her back, Phyllis glanced at her watch. Seven o'clock. Long past time to leave. She buzzed Dickie still cocooned in his office.

"Major Simpson?"

"Yes, Phyllis. What is it?"

"If you don't need anything further, I'm going home."

"I've got a few letters, but they can wait until tomorrow. Would you come in to get them, please?"

"Certainly."

When she opened the door, a short man sat across the desk from Dickie. With a hat on his lap, he kept his gaze on Simpson so she couldn't see his face. When Dickie handed her the letters, she glanced at the man's profile—no one she knew and they weren't introduced. She was used to that actually; it was none of her business who Dickie did business with, but generally she knew his visitors. She thought she had seen him around the Embassy, but couldn't be sure. This man was short, dark in coloring with a gabardine trench coat. His hat was not a fedora, as most men she knew wore, but a homburg. Huh. That made him stand out in her mind as something unique.

Be curious of anything out of place.

As fast as Amy's request came back to her, however, Phyllis tucked it aside. It was nothing, just business as usual in the American Embassy. Dickie knew what he was doing—she bade him goodnight, stacked the letters in her inbox for the next day and prepared to leave.

She walked down the street to catch the London Underground, commonly called the tube, at Marble Arch Station. While humming quickly along with other travelers, Phyllis mused how the subway system had been used during the Blitz. Those times for extreme measures had passed, but would never be forgotten. She wondered how horrible it must have been to sleep in the smelly confines of the underground subway with hundreds of people stacked in like cordwood. There were constant fears of bombs hitting water mains or gas lines which would and occasionally did flood the tube and kill English citizens trying to escape the terror, only to find a new one. She shivered knowing people may have died in the very area where she was sitting.

The ride was fast with her thoughts focused on events at the Embassy the past few days. Getting off at Holborn Station, Phyllis walked the short distance to Covent Gardens where she was meeting an old friend.

Ann Fletcher was the retired secretary to William Bradley, the Military Attache before Ronald Lawrence. Col. Bradley had been in the office since World War I and, rumor had it, wasn't thrilled to have to go through another world war overseas. He was homesick and ready to leave, but it still took the President a year to find his replacement. Bradley's secretary, Ann, had become a true Anglophile and remained at the Embassy a while longer after his retirement from the service. England was still at war so Ann chose to stay, even though she wasn't ready to retire. She was living in a small flat above a bookstore in Covent Gardens and had a pot of tea brewing when she answered Phyllis' knock.

"Phyllis! Lovely to see you again. How are you?"

She bussed both Phyllis' cheeks and took her arm to draw her into the sitting room. The "best" room in the flat had a coal fire from a side stove, since gas was at a premium and often unavailable. Phyllis noticed a box of candles, a leftover from the constant air raids of a year or so back.

"Good, Ann. Thanks for seeing me."

"I was surprised to hear you wanted to come over and so close to blackout time."

She took Phyllis' coat and went into the kitchen. "Have a seat. I'll be right back."

Phyllis sat on a couch that had obviously lost a few springs when she sunk deeply into it. Glancing around the comfortable room, she noted the radio in one corner far away from windows with blackout curtains and crisscrossed bits of tape.

"Do you still need tape on the windows, Ann?" she called out.

Ann walked in with a silver tray, steaming teapot and cups of fine china.

"Not so much anymore, but we still get the occasional buzz bomb so I'm not willing to take any chances. How about where you live?"

"I'm closer to the Embassy, around West Kensington and we've seen our share of action since I've lived here, that's true."

"I've heard about that historic row house by the bridge where you managed to get a room. What famous person lived there?"

"Samuel Taylor Coleridge."

"Ah, yes. Seven Addison Bridge Place. How on earth did you get a room there?"

"The usual way—someone I knew talked to someone they knew." Phyllis smiled. "Pure luck, I'm sure."

Ann set the tray down on a small table by the couch. She poured hot water into a cup using a strainer to catch loose tealeaves.

Handing it to Phyllis, she remarked, "I have sugar rations but alas, no milk. All we get is the powder variety which…"

"Tastes terrible, I know. Thank you." Phyllis added a sugar cube, stirred the cup and took a sip.

"How is it?"

"Very nice, Ann." She tilted her head. "Lapsang Souchong?"

Ann smiled, fixed her cup. "You know your teas and yes, I should have lemon with it but you know how impossible it is to get fresh fruit."

"I do indeed."

Both women took a sip of their tea and looked over at one another.

"I'm also out of biscuits."

Phyllis reached into her pocket for a tiny silver packet. "I figured as much so I brought these to add to the tea."

Ann's smile lit up the room. "Shortbread? Wherever…"

"We at the Embassy have our ways but if you must know, they're from New Zealand."

"Our shipping lanes must be open that way then."

"They say the war's almost over."

Ann opened the packet and took out a small square biscuit. A delicate nibble made her face look almost childlike. "I'd forgotten how good these are. Thank you so much for brightening my day."

"You're welcome, Ann."

"But I'm sure you didn't come all this way just to make sure your old mentor had a few biscuits."

Phyllis studied Ann Fletcher as she sipped her tea. Short curly hair framed a face with little crinkles around her dark eyes. She set her cup down, placed folded hands in her lap to stare back at Phyllis. A decorative pin topped her plain cotton blouse with a Peter Pan collar. Her skirt was belted and she sported a watch on her left wrist. She could have been any number of English women working in a factory, but Phyllis knew that belied her native intelligence, her solid ability to tell fact from fiction, right from wrong. Ann had taken her under her wing when Phyllis had first arrived at the Embassy. When many gave her the cold shoulder, Ann gave her bits of advice to keep her on the right track. She trusted this woman's opinion more than anyone else's in all of Britain.

Phyllis grinned. "You can still cut through to the meat pretty fast, can't you?"

Ann nodded. "As much as I'd like to think this is a social call, it isn't. Correct?"

"Afraid not."

She must have known Phyllis' reluctance to talk of things she probably shouldn't. Ann sought her comfort with the following declaration.

"I was young when I began my career in diplomacy. I had various jobs in Washington before being assigned overseas, but you know all that," Ann said congenially. Pouring another cup of tea for them both, she continued. "I was thrilled to be assigned to the American Embassy here in London and to Col. Bradley, in particular. He had been in London for several years already and had a stellar reputation. I remember when he told me, 'A military attache is a military expert who is attached to a diplomatic mission.' When I asked him what his job was, he told me he would monitor various issues related to areas of intervention."

She stopped, sipped her tea. "It didn't make much sense to me until I got into the nitty gritty of military intelligence and found I had a knack for it." Nodding, she added, "You do too, my dear."

"I assume you've heard what's happened at the Embassy."

"Yes."

"So you still have contacts in and about the Embassy."

"I do."

"I need your help."

"What do you need? And be precise."

But Phyllis couldn't do that. Instead she crept up on what she really wanted. "I worked in the Pentagon in the Purchases Division for a while until I was transferred to the War Department where I worked as a secretary."

"But that wasn't enough for you, was it?"

"No. A transfer to the American Embassy in London came up eight months ago and I applied knowing what I would be doing is stenographer work."

"That's important work."

"To be sure. I was in charge of files of over two hundred officers: leave, temporary leave and detached service. I had to contact officers to get necessary information and I wrote travel orders. That was before the office of assistant military attache needed a secretary."

"And I recommended you because you were such a hard worker."

"Thank you."

"Which brings us up to date, Phyllis. The time has come for you to tell me what you're doing here."

Phyllis took a sip of her cooling tea, set the cup down. When she opened her mouth, even she was surprised at the words that marched out.

"When you worked for Col. Bradley, were you ever suspicious of anyone?"

"Oh, everyone, my dear." She smiled. "It's safer to trust no one and keep your mouth shut. You learn a lot more that way." She stared for a moment into the fire. "You know, some people think secretaries are not very bright, but that's not true, is it?"

Phyllis waited. When Ann added nothing further, she asked, "You're not going to give me any advice, are you?"

"No, dear, but I will give you a name."

"A name?"

"Yes."

"What name?"

Ann locked eyes with Phyllis. "Salamander."

Phyllis looked incredulously at Ann until she sneezed unexpectedly.

"God bless you."

Ann stood and walked to a cabinet to pluck out a small box from a drawer.

"Thank you, but 'salamander'? What does that mean?"

From the box, Ann took out a handkerchief, handing it over to Phyllis. After she'd blotted her nose, Phyllis handed it back.

"No, you keep it. You may need it again."

Phyllis rose to leave. "I need to get going. It's blackout and my landlady will blow a gasket if I'm not home soon."

"Take care, my dear, and trust your instincts. You'll be fine."

But Phyllis didn't feel fine walking toward the subway station after leaving Ann's flat. She sneezed again, bringing the hanky back up to her nose. Before putting it back into her purse, she noticed something red in the corner and brought the hanky closer to see. Initials. SR? Whose initials were those and why had Ann given her someone else's hanky? She nearly threw it in the closest waste bin, but somehow couldn't do it.

SR? Had Ann been trying to tell her something and if so, what the devil did it mean?

* * *

CHAPTER 9

From Holborn Station, Phyllis rode the tube to West Kensington and walked the rest of the way to her home. It was a chilly night and she'd buttoned her coat snugly before turning on her small flashlight, so she wouldn't trip on the uneven sidewalk. Her section of London, as were all sections of London, was as black as black could be. Every house had dark curtains covering their windows; some people had even painted or put cardboard up. Streetlights were switched off or dimmed and shielded to deflect the light downward. Even cars and traffic lights were fitted with slotted covers to deflect the beam down.

But apparently the battery was getting low on her flashlight and she looked right into the fading light, smacking it with her hand to get the battery to work. A bobby walking across the street called out to her, "Mind your torch!" She guiltily aimed the small light towards the sidewalk and hurried to the row house where she lived. Going in the front door, she heard Mrs. Stewart on the telephone.

"As sure as I'm living, there was another car accident right in front of my house today!"

"Hello, Mrs. Stewart," Phyllis said walking by to go up the staircase.

The tiny landlady put a hand over the receiver. "Phyllis, there's a letter for you on the dining table."

As Phyllis went into the dining room, Mrs. Stewart continued, "That's right, Edna. I can't believe the number of accidents during blackout time. Sure, it's necessary so the bombers can't see us, but one of my girls was nearly hit this evening!"

The letter was from Phyllis' sister, Mary Ellen, and contained the usual pleas for more money and for her to come home. A picture included of her father tugged her heartstrings, but there was no way she could get home just yet. If the war was over in the coming months, maybe she could make it happen. Until then, she'd have to continue feeling guilty for not helping her family more, complicating her strong desire to help her country and England in the war effort. It was a real push-pull and not a problem to be remedied any time soon.

Changing out of work clothes, she put on her new coveralls. They were all the rage thanks to the 'Rosie the Riveter' clothing made for women working in the factories, and made her way back downstairs to the kitchen.

High jinks at Seven Addison Bridge Place were loud and boisterous. Surprisingly, all four of her roommates were home and clanking pots and pans in the kitchen, causing Mrs. Stewart to retreat to her flat.

"What? No date tonight, Norma?"

A perky redhead turned her way. "Hey, Phyllis! When did you get home?"

"Just now."

"And I have no date because all the boys had to go back to base."

"But," interrupted blonde Doris with a grin, "we've been invited to go up to Ipswich for a dance this weekend. Interested?"

"Hmm," Phyllis tapped her chin. "Let's see—would I rather stay home to do my laundry or go to a rousing good time with the 474th Squadron? Tough choice."

The girls around her laughed. "We're leaving tomorrow afternoon, Phyllis. See if you can get off a little early," added Mildred.

"Maybe the Red Cross gives you girls spare time," she said to Mildred and Doris, "but Embassy doesn't cut us much slack."

"I'll agree with that," said Lorraine coolly appraising the ingredients on the table. "Looks like we have enough for vegetable soup. Who's going to make it?"

Everyone pointed at Phyllis. "Hey, I cooked last night."

"And the night before that and the night before that." Norma lifted playful brows at Mildred. "You're the best cook and we knew you'd complain…"

"…So we got you something," finished Mildred. Bringing a small package wrapped in butcher paper out from behind her back, she handed it over.

"What is it?" When she opened the package, Phyllis' lips parted in surprise. "Sausages! Where did you get these?"

"Mrs. Stewart's butcher got them in after weeks of waiting for supplies. Isn't it great?"

"Wonderful!" She turned to her roommates. "So naturally you want me to put them in the soup?"

"Please," they all said at once.

Laughing, Phyllis went to work dicing the vegetables into bite size pieces. Lorraine got the soup pot going on the stove while the rest of the girls wandered into the dining room to set the table. "It'll be a while before it's ready, someone turn on the radio," she called out.

"Got it!" a cheery voice responded.

As music filled the air, the girls in the dining room kicked off their shoes to dance a fast jitterbug. Amidst laughter and high stepping, a more ominous sound began to drown out the music. Recognizing it at once, the women froze where they stood for a split second before frenzied activity burst out.

"Duck!" Lorraine yelled.

As the telltale droning sound died, the more terrifying silence made everyone cringe. Too late for a shelter somewhere, everyone, including Mrs. Stewart, crouched under tables, behind sofas. Someone sped off to the bathroom just as the buzz bomb exploded somewhere outside the dining room window. The force of the blast

51

blew the blackout shade to the ceiling with shards of glass and remnants of the destroyed window raining down on them all.

It might have been only a few minutes. It might have been hours. When time stands still, there's no clock handy and it couldn't tell you anything anyway.

It had been a very close call. Phyllis' ears rang as she continued to crouch in a corner of the kitchen holding her hands over her ears. It was a while before anyone stirred. Finally, Lorraine stood up.

"Everyone okay?" She glanced around. "I miss the All Clear signals they used to do."

Norma, closest to the window, moved out from under the shredded blackout shade. She and Mildred shifted cautiously brushing debris from their clothes and hair. Mrs. Stewart looked shell-shocked, so Lorraine led her back to her flat.

"I'm okay," called out Doris who had made it the bathroom just before the blast hit.

Phyllis looked down at the squished sausages on the floor. "Everyone still want sausage in their soup?" Half-hearted chuckles met her little joke and the women moved into the kitchen. "Let's get cleanup organized and I'll finish cooking."

For the next few hours, the women combined forces to renew a semblance of normalcy in the house. New sounds filled the air with chattering voices, a vacuum cleaner running, mops dragging across floors and rags wiping every surface available. The house was soon cleaner after the bomb blast than before it. A hastily assembled tarpaulin now hung in the dining room. Chattering turned to chuckles and, although shaken, the women were ready to assume life again. But in the back of everyone's mind was the fact that another bomb could be behind the first. Although, Phyllis and her roommates talked, they were listening too.

Dinner was strained, but still happy. They were alive and that's all that mattered.

* * *

CHAPTER 10

The trip to Ipswich that weekend was fun-filled. Phyllis and her roommates had had to switch trains twice, but it was worth it to watch the train chug slowly out of London, away from their worries for a little while. They knew many of the boys in the 474th squadron at the P51 fighter base, almost three hours north of London in the English countryside. Chugging through the pastoral setting, Phyllis was surprised to see cattle roaming the landscape and mile after mile of farmland. No pollution from city traffic, but the rumbling of the fighter planes from the nearby base may have been sound pollution for farmers in the area. She knew they didn't have the incessant bombing that London still endured, but war was war. Its effects came in different forms.

A wing of the base hospital had been opened for the girls to use for the weekend. At first it seemed strange to be assembling a makeshift bedroom out of tray tables and hospital beds, but the atmosphere was uplifting, and the dance that night made all inconveniences seem trivial.

The boys had gotten several of their own to play for the dance and soon the tunes of Cole Porter, Ira Gershwin, Frank Sinatra and the Andrews Sisters enticed everyone to 'cut a rug'. After too much gin and hours of swing, jitterbugging and slow dancing with very willing soldiers, Phyllis and Lorraine eventually collapsed in their hospital beds with sore feet and beaming smiles.

"What time is it?"

"Who cares, Phyl?"

"I want to kid our roommates when they fall in bed for staying out so late."

"It must be around two a.m."

"Thought so." Phyllis peeled off her soggy blouse and threw it on a chair. "For this I bought new glad rags."

"Don't be a wet blanket. I had a blast."

"Me too. Did you hear what Sparky and Dave told everyone we would be doing tomorrow?"

Lorraine unbuttoned her skirt. "I shudder to ask."

"A picnic in the countryside."

"Guess they're not working tomorrow," she shrugged.

"Turn off the light, will you? I can't move from this bed."

An hour later, Phyllis was awakened when the rest of their group finally made it to bed. Before her eyes closed, she saw an older man stoking the fire in their room and she would wake to see him again that night. What a generous thing to do. Her mind was slipping into unconsciousness when her final thought was about the bravery and generosity of the English people. And everyone else in the world who had suffered enough.

On the train home, she was dozing when she overheard Doris and Mildred gossiping in the seat in front of her.

"So then Beverly told Palmer who told me that there just weren't enough girls to keep up with all the boys from the base."

"Didn't you tell her that we've had the boys over to the house probably three times in the last three months? Mrs. Stewart about tore her hair at…"

"Yes, we mentioned that, but when all the trouble started at the Embassy…"

"What trouble?"

"Oh, you know. That lieutenant colonel what's-his-name was arrested for something…"

"Sure but that didn't damper any of our fun."

Mildred's voice lowered. "Yes, it has. Didn't you hear?"

"Hear what?" asked Doris in an equally low tone.

"Palmer told Bev who told me that his secretary overdosed on sleeping pills."

"What?"

Phyllis bolted upright.

"That's right and I'm surprised Phyllis and Lorraine were even allowed to come with us this weekend. Why, it's…"

"What happened, Mildred?" Phyllis leaned over the seat in front of her, practically in Mildred's face.

She shrank back. "I thought you knew."

"Tell me everything you know…right now."

"Well, someone told me on the train coming out here and…"

"Who?"

Mildred looked confused. "I'm not sure exactly, we were talking about a lot of things with several people on the train."

"Wait a minute," Phyllis said impatiently. She dashed around to the row in front of her and bumped Doris out of her seat. "Sorry, I need this."

"Okay, fine."

Once Phyllis was in the seat next to Mildred, she waved a hand. "Go on, continue."

"It's like I said—some secretary overdosed on sleeping pills."

"What secretary?"

"Um…I'm not sure. The man who was arrested…"

"Lt. Col. Ronald Lawrence."

"Okay, I guess that's the one."

"Was it his secretary?"

Mildred looked sheepishly at Phyllis, then at Doris who was standing in the aisle. "I think so. Someone told me she took too many pills."

"Was it a suicide attempt?"

Mildred shook her head. "Honestly, Phyl, I just don't know anything else. I thought you knew, so I haven't mentioned it before. Did you know her?"

Phyllis inhaled a ragged breath. "Yes, I knew her. I *know* her. She works at the Embassy. How could I not know her?"

"I'm so sorry."

Phyllis rose and wandered back three rows to where Lorraine was dozing. She motioned for the girl next to her to leave and sat down next to her. She shook Lorraine's arm.

"Lorraine."

"Mmm...."

"Lorraine!"

Her eyes blinked open. "What? I've had six hours of sleep in three days. What's so important?" She blinked drowsy eyes at Phyllis.

"Amy Broadbent tried to commit suicide. Did you know that?"

"What?" She rubbed her eyes. "What, Phyllis?"

"Amy tried to kill herself."

"What? Who told you that?"

"I overheard Mildred and Doris speaking. They heard it from someone on the train on the way to Ipswich. Why, we've been drinking and dancing while all the time..."

"No," Lorraine put a hand in front of her. "Don't do that. Don't blame yourself for something we had no control over."

Phyllis leaned back in her seat, shook her head briskly. "I don't understand. Why would she do it?"

"First off," Lorraine began, "you don't really know what's happened. You know how Mildred gets things wrong. Maybe what she heard was wrong."

"And maybe what she heard was right."

"I'm sorry it happened, but what difference does it make?"

Good question. Phyllis hadn't told her friend about Amy's solemn request—to find out what was really going on at the Embassy. No one knew any more than when Lawrence had been arrested several days ago.

Tears leaked out her eyes. With tears sliding down her cheeks, Phyllis wiped them away getting angrier with each passing moment. Lorraine nudged her.

"What are you thinking? You have a pretty mad face going on."

Phyllis glanced left to right, then leaned in to whisper in Lorraine's ear.

"You know I'm not an impulsive person, right?" Lorraine nodded. "And you know I wouldn't do something without thinking it over."

Lorraine whispered back, "You think things to death."

"Right, so here's what I know: Amy asked me to look into why Lt. Col. Lawrence was arrested for espionage. She said it was all rubbish."

"And you believe her?

"Yes. I do now."

Lorraine's jaw dropped. "Why?"

"She tried to kill herself. She believes so much in Lawrence's innocence that she begged me to help her."

"What did you say?"

"I said no."

Lorraine grabbed Phyllis' shoulders. "Don't go blaming yourself for what happened to Amy."

She stared back at her. "Who else is there to blame?"

They exchanged a long look between them until Lorraine finally nodded. "Okay. I know there's no changing your mind once it's made up, so what's next?"

Phyllis extended her hand. "Are you in?"

She chuckled, put her hand in Phyllis'. "Of course, I'm in, you ninny. What will you do?"

A slow smile creased Phyllis' face. "I'm going to keep my eyes and ears wide open. If I hear anything, I'm going to the military police."

"What do you want me to do?"

"Stay tuned. I'm taking a scary step into the unknown this week."

"Be careful."

What was she getting herself into?

* * *

CHAPTER 11

Phyllis went to see Amy at the hospital the next day. She was asleep, so Phyllis parked on a chair next to her bed, waiting for her to awaken. Glancing around the sterile environment with white walls, beeping machines and tubes running into Amy's pale arms did little to cheer her. Amy seemed to be breathing normally, but little color had left her face looking wan. A nurse came in to check her vital signs, smiled at Phyllis and left. As she was leaving, Amy woke sleepily.

"Amy? It's Phyllis."

Amy turned her head towards the sound of her voice. "Phyllis? You're here?"

"Yes, I am. Are you all right?"

She shook her head and hid her face in the blanket. "You shouldn't be here."

"Why not?"

"...I...I'm so ashamed."

Phyllis scooted her chair closer. "No, I'm ashamed, Amy."

"Why should you be ashamed?"

"Please look at me."

She waited until she could see Amy's face. Once springy curls were matted to her scalp. She reached over to clasp an ice-cold hand.

"What?"

"Remember what you said to me at Angel's?"

"You should forget I said anything. I was just babbling."

"No, you weren't. You had a feeling that something's wrong and I'm beginning to get those feelings too."

"You are?"

"Yeah." Phyllis squeezed the hand. "I'm ashamed that I didn't take you seriously at the time."

"Phyllis—"

"No, let me finish."

"I pushed aside any notion that there could be some kind of infiltration at the Embassy because I didn't want to believe it. That means someone I know and respect may be committing acts of treason. It's not a small notion and frankly, scares me to death."

Amy struggled to sit up.

"Lie back, it's fine. Just talk to me."

"Okay." She lay back and quieted for a moment. "What do you want to know? I'll tell you anything, if it will help Mr. Lawrence."

Phyllis checked to see if another patient was in the room, then closed the door. Satisfied that they were alone, she still leaned closer to Amy.

"Did you ever hear Ronnie use the word 'salamander'?"

"What? In the office? Somewhere in the Embassy?"

"Yes."

Amy shook her head. "No, I don't think so. What does it mean besides a kind of small reptile?"

"Do you know anyone with the initials SR?"

Again, she shook her head. "No. Are these questions meaningful?"

Phyllis softly sighed, disappointment flooding through her. "I think they're meaningful to someone, I just haven't met the right person yet."

"I'm sorry I can't help you. Anything else?"

"Did Ronnie ever have a visitor, a short man wearing a gabardine coat and homburg?"

Amy raised a hand to rub her nose. The IV line in her arm crinkled making a machine start beeping. "Oh, great. Not again."

A nurse hurried in to straighten the line and turn off the alert. "You okay?"

"I just moved, that's all."

"Good enough." The young nurse smiled benevolently at Phyllis before leaving.

"You need to get out of here."

"I'm being shipped back to the States."

"Really?" Phyllis shrugged. "It's probably for the best. They say the war's almost over anyway. When are you leaving?"

"As soon as I'm discharged and on military transport, if there's room."

"Please keep in touch, if you can. I'll let you know if I find out anything."

A sweet smile erased the worry lines in Amy's face. "You believe me?"

"I think you're right—there *is* a rotten apple in the Embassy. I didn't want to believe it, but I'm not one for denial. The next step is action."

"I'll let you know if I think of anything else."

"Any small detail could help, Amy. You were with Ronnie so much, anything unique must stand out in your mind."

Amy was quiet for several minutes twisting her blanket tightly. When she turned to see Phyllis better, the machine began beeping again. Amy moved to her original position and the irritating noise stopped.

"You asked me about some man in a homburg?"

Phyllis straightened. "Yes, do you know who he is?"

"He's been in a few times, now that I think of it, over the past two years but Mr. Lawrence never introduced us. I'm not sure who he is."

"You never thought it odd that Ronnie didn't introduce you to him?"

She scrunched her downcast eyes. "I'm not sure but I think he was a holdover from the past administration. I got the feeling Ronnie didn't introduce him because he was unimportant, pesky almost."

"Pesky?"

"Yes, like an offending fly Ronnie was trying to brush away, so I didn't think much about him."

"But you say he was in a few times."

She nodded. "I remember the homburg because it seemed out of place." Her face suddenly brightened. "That's one of the things I told you to watch for, isn't it? You don't know who he is either?"

"No," Phyllis' eyes narrowed, "but I mean to find out."

She stood by Amy's bed, reached for her hand. "Please let me know how you are when you get back to the States. Where's home, by the way?"

"Just outside of Washington, D.C. in Georgetown."

"Good. Take care." Phyllis picked up her purse and took a step towards the door.

"And Phyllis?"

She looked back. "What, Amy?"

"Go get 'em."

They grinned at one another with sunshine flooding the space, lightening the austere atmosphere.

"I promise."

* * *

CHAPTER 12

Major Simpson kept most of the staff working late all the next week. Buzz bombs had dropped with more frequency, but less accuracy. Several had dropped by the Embassy, one hitting the front of the apartments across the street but luckily, no one was killed. Streets sustained much of the damage creating a tense atmosphere with flaring tempers. Employees of the Embassy were on edge and wound tight. Dickie was out of the office more than he was in, keeping Phyllis hopping with several important tasks. And of course, everything needed to be done now.

He seemed more worried than usual, but Phyllis chalked it up to being new in the job and probably overwhelmed. One night, exhausted after staying until eleven for last minute changes in some of Dickie's have-to-be-done-now reports, Phyllis fell asleep on a couch in the staff lounge, around the corner from the Officers' Mess. She had intended to just rest her eyes for a few minutes, but the couch was so soft and her feet were aching. After stretching out and cuddling into the comfy cushions, her eyes popped open and she hurriedly sought her watch to see what time it was. *Twelve o'clock?* Goodness! She'd been asleep for an hour!

Phyllis ran back upstairs to her office wondering why the heck no one woke her up, yet happy no one had caught her napping. The maintenance staff had come and gone, and the place was quiet as a tomb. With light from a full moon reflecting through the Embassy windows, she could make her way with little difficulty. Her office light had been turned off, Dickie probably assumed she'd left, and she began putting away work for the next day. That's when she heard Dickie's voice in his darkened office. He was still here.

Tiptoeing to the slightly open door, she cautiously peaked in. He was on the phone speaking in low tones with his feet up on his desk, his tie and jacket tossed carelessly on a chair. She began to retreat when she heard him plain as day.

"...From the salamander fund? What? No...that's not what I was led to believe." He paused for a moment, then spoke again so low she couldn't hear until, "Oh, all right. Let me check." He put the phone down swinging his legs off the desk.

Salamander? Phyllis froze for a split second before stepping back quickly, nearly tripping on a box by the door. What to do? He might be suspicious that she was still here, so she ducked under her desk, curling inward as tightly as possible. The instant she closed her eyes and prayed for invisibility, Dickie strode into her office standing right by her chair. If he'd looked down, he would have seen her hiding and asked her what the heck she was doing. Or maybe he'd be angry that she had overheard him. *What was salamander,* she was dying to ask. At any rate, he shuffled through various papers in her inbox, picked something up and walked back into his office not bothering to shut the door between their offices.

Great. Now she'd be stuck here until he left.

In the dead of night with very few sounds, she could hear his voice clearly. He picked up the phone.

"No, I accidentally put it on Phyllis' desk. No...no. Absolutely not...She wouldn't understand it. Okay...Why? All right. That seems excessive but I'll burn it now."

Burn it? Why would he need to burn anything? Embassy procedure dictated any materials to be discarded were to be shredded. Burning indicated a heightened sense of secrecy and was perhaps the reason he was still here at this late hour.

In a few minutes, her nostrils picked up the scent of smoke. She stayed hidden under the desk longer than necessary after Dickie left the office. The heavy front door closed long ago when she pushed out from under the desk, stretching cramped legs and prickly feet. Stepping softly, Phyllis walked into Dickie's office, nose upturned to locate the source of the smoke. His waste bin contained ashes and several small remnants of paper. She reluctantly reached in to pluck out the paper with shaky fingers soon coated with ash.

What's this? Numbers? Places? The scraps were unreadable, but it had to be incriminating for Dickie to burn it. *What was he up to?*

After tonight, she would be fully on guard and watchful in the office of the Military Attache. With an unidentified visitor and ashes in the waste bin, Phyllis knew the game was afoot.

* * *

CHAPTER 13

Lorraine sat at a small table towards the back of the pub. The Blue Anchor was a mess on the outside and didn't look habitable, but it was open due to resilient Brits desperate to keep as many pubs in business as possible through the never-ending war. Tarps were nailed to the windows and a grimy blanket covered the doorway. A makeshift bar of worn boards kept hands at bay for fear of slivers until glasses of ale were poured and grabbed immediately, slivers or no. Lorraine and other patrons preferred this bar to Angel's because it had already been bombed, so there was little fear it would be bombed again. Even so, there was nothing left to destroy. Tables and chairs had to be shuffled to one side every night as strong men rolled kegs of beer into place behind the bar.

It was a work in progress and a huge source of pride to the establishment's clientele. Lorraine was only half-kidding when she told Phyllis a password was needed to get in. Generally, there was standing room only and she'd lucked out finding two unoccupied chairs. It probably helped that she'd met up with the bartender once, a cute bearded Scot with a shock of red hair and a pouting lip whenever she turned him down for another encounter. She sighed at the sleepy man at her table.

"You've had enough, Henry."

"S-says who?"

"Says me." She shook her head at the good-looking man with eyes half-closed propping up his head with his hands on the table. Not always successfully. Lorraine had met Henry McKinnon at a State Department function a few months back and she noticed his loose lips almost immediately. She'd pried them open tonight with a few too many beers on purpose.

Raising her hand to the Scot behind the bar brought over another glass. She was in this far, why not go a bit farther?

"Sure ye should be a-fillin' this one with more of our finest, Lorraine? He looks a wee bit wobbly."

"He's fine, Malcolm. Thanks." Looking doubtful, he left the foamy glass on her table.

"Here you go, Henry. Drink up."

Henry's brown eyes glazed over at the sight of a fresh drink at his elbow. But he must have been seeing double and reached for the wrong one. Lorraine grabbed his hand to place the glass in it. After he gulped a quarter of the ale leaving foam all over his mouth and chin, she wiped him clean with a napkin before leaning in.

"So Henry…"

His watery eyes tried to focus. "Whatsh up, honey? Wanna kiss?" Henry puckered his lips with eyes closed tight. She stifled a laugh.

"Not right now, but I do want something. Henry?" She shook his shoulder. "Can you hear me?"

Nodding, he grabbed for his glass, nearly dumping it into her lap.

"Hey! Watch it!"

"Sorry, sorry…"

"Henry, sweetie."

He smiled a baby-faced smile in her direction, but she wasn't sure he could actually see her any longer. No matter.

"Henry, what's the buzz at State these days about our new military attaché. You know," she poked him in the arm, "Dick Simpson."

His cheerful composure slipped. "Simpson. Whatanidiot. He better, *hic,* watch his step."

"What do you mean by that?"

"Jus' wha' I said." Henry's head went down on the table and he was out for the count.

"Great," sighed Lorraine. "Just when he was getting interesting."

A shadow fell across Henry and the table.

"Need some help here, miss?"

"No, I'm fine. Thanks, mister..."

The tall man stuck out his hand. "Joe Schneider at your service." He angled his head towards the sleeping man. "I work with Henry at the State Department. It looks like you could use some help."

Lorraine smoothed her pageboy, glanced around the packed pub. She was ready to ditch Henry and find someone new for a few hours. Curfew would be soon and she wanted to have a little fun. Henry hadn't cut it tonight and he certainly hadn't told her what she wanted to know. She looked up into the enquiring gaze of handsome Joe Schneider.

"You know where he lives? Could you take him home?"

His quick smile seemed...something, she couldn't put her finger on what.

"I do. How about..." He leaned a hand on her table. "I take him off your hands in exchange for..."

"For what?" She picked up her purse, fished around in it. "I don't have any cigarettes for trade tonight."

"I'd like something else."

She snorted. "Nice try but you're not my type, Joe." She waved a hand. "Feel free to take Henry home or leave him, I don't care."

"I've seen you in here with a lovely lady I'd like to meet. That's my price for the exchange."

"What lovely lady?" she frowned. "I've been in here with lots of friends."

"She has curly brown hair cut to about here," he indicated his shoulder. "She's pretty and I'd like to make her acquaintance."

Frowning, she looked him over. "How do I know you aren't Jack the Ripper?"

The wattage of his smile increased. "You friends with Malcolm? So am I, so ask him about me. I'm fairly well-known here as a nice guy and generous tipper."

When Lorraine continued to stare at him, he raised three fingers. "I promise I'm not Jack the Ripper."

She softened somewhat and beckoned to Malcolm. After the bartender verified that Joe was okay, Lorraine nodded her head. "Okay, I think you're talking about my friend, Phyllis. About 5'5", brown eyes, worn-out trench coat?"

"That's her. Could you introduce us?"

She stood, helped Henry to his feet. When Joe took him, Lorraine tapped him on the shoulder. "Seven Addison Bridge Place in West Kensington tomorrow night at eight. We're having a little party for the boys from the 474th in town from Ipswich."

"I'll be there," he beamed. "Thanks, Lorraine."

"I won't even ask how you know my name."

His grin never faltered. "Malcolm told me."

She wasn't sure Malcolm had, but he seemed all right, so she felt Phyllis would be safe—and on neutral territory where all her roommates could stand guard.

"Tomorrow then." He hoisted drunken Henry up and staggered towards the doorway.

"How you getting him home?" she called out.

"Taxi. See you soon."

With few misgivings, Lorraine took out her tube of lipstick, freshened her lips. Malcolm waved to her from the bar and she trotted over, forgetting about Joe Schneider on her way over to flirt with the cute Scot.

The fat was in the proverbial fire.

* * *

CHAPTER 14

Mrs. Stewart wouldn't approve. Luckily, she was visiting her sister in Stratford so the girls had the house to themselves. Rather they were sharing the house with what seemed like most of the boys from the fighter base up in Ipswich.

It was the first wild party they'd had in months. There was a major mess in the living room with cups and glasses everywhere, none of them broken—yet. Mildred and Norma had dashed next door to borrow ice cubes from Mrs. Smith, a friend of Mrs. Stewart. When she'd asked what was going on over there, the girls smiled demurely and remarked they just had a few friends over. Mrs. Smith had huffed at that and they knew Mrs. Stewart would be informed as soon as humanly possible. Until then, they would eat, drink and be merry!

Two or three bottles of champagne were opened and one bottle of V.O. No one was sure who had brought the Canadian whiskey, but the rowdy group was happy that someone did.

"Whew! I haven't had anything to drink since—"

"...Our trip to the base last weekend?"

Phyllis laughed, took another sip of champagne. "Something like that. Say, Lorraine. Who's that handsome guy who keeps staring at me?"

She glanced in the direction Phyllis was looking. "Oh, that's Joe Schneider."

"Who's he?"

"Some State Department friend of Henry's."

"You seeing Henry again?"

She shrugged, pushed hair off her shoulder. "Off and on."

"Who invited him?"

Lorraine's eyes widened. "Oh, I did. I forgot. He did me a favor by taking a very snockered Henry home last night and I promised him I'd introduce you."

"Why would you do that?"

"He wants to meet you. Guess he's got a minor crush or something. Humor him tonight. Malcolm says he's okay."

Laughing again, Phyllis reached over to pour a little more champagne in her glass. "Fine. Introduce us then. I haven't got all night."

"Actually, sweetie, you do."

Chuckling, they headed in Joe's direction. He immediately broke off the conversation he was having with Mildred, Sparky and Dave to meet Lorraine and Phyllis in the middle of the room. He put out his hand as Lorraine made introductions.

"Joe Schneider, State Department, meet Phyllis Bowman, American Embassy. Who says government agencies can't communicate?"

"Funny," said Phyllis. "Nice to meet you, Joe."

"The pleasure is all mine. I've been wanting to meet you for a while."

Lorraine stepped away. "And this is where I leave you." Neither watched her go.

"Why is that? I'm a lowly secretary at the Embassy. No one of great importance."

"I guess that's in the eye of the beholder, Miss Bowden."

She laughed. "I've already called you Joe, so I believe it's appropriate for you to call me Phyllis."

They shook hands longer than was necessary. He waved a hand toward the dining room. "It's not as noisy in there as in the kitchen and parlor. Shall we?"

Nodding, Phyllis made for the dining room, dodging rambunctious fliers on the way. Val and Cliff each had two drinks apiece complaining about the lack of ice. They must be out...again.

72

"What happened here?" Joe reached out to touch the enormous tarpaulin covering the space where the window used to be.

"I'm sure you can guess—a buzz bomb."

"Of course. I'm over by Covent Gardens and the house two doors down was hit a couple of nights ago."

She shuddered. "When will this war be over?"

"Even when it is, some bomber won't get the message in time and the destruction will continue for a while longer."

"I can't wait until it's over."

"You and me both. So tell me, Phyllis, where's home?"

"I live in Arlington, Virginia, outside of Washington, D.C."

He nodded. "Sure, I've been there. Beautiful area. You have family there?"

"My whole family—my sister and her family, plus my father. I was living with him when this transfer came through to London."

"He probably didn't want you to go, but…"

"…There's a war on," she finished looking down at the floor. "He isn't well and I…ah, I haven't been as good a daughter as I should be."

"Let me guess: he's sick and your sister is pushing you to come home to help with his care."

Her jaw dropped. "How do you know that? Been reading my mail?"

He chuckled. "Hardly. I'm snoopy and asked a few people about you."

"You are snoopy."

"Guilty as charged. I was just interested in meeting you, hope you don't mind."

She took another sip and glanced up at him. "As long as that's as far as your snooping goes. I don't want a stalker."

"And you won't have one. Honestly…" His smile seemed innocent, but there was something familiar about him.

"Have we met before?"

73

He shook his head before she finished her question. "I'd've remembered, trust me."

He was handsome with dark wavy hair and piercing eyes that reminded her of some silent film star. Valentino maybe…without the makeup, of course.

"What's the smirk about? Am I funny?"

No, you're very attractive. "I think I need more champagne."

"Yes, ma'am. Be right back."

They spent the rest of the party talking, dodging more tipsy fliers and perky roommates until it was close to two in the morning. After the whiskey and champagne were gone, the squadron boys sadly began their farewells. Joe touched her hand.

"Could I take you to dinner tomorrow?"

"Well, I…"

"Because Mick at Angel's has gotten in some sausage, so John's cooking—"

"Toad in the Hole?"

He grinned. "You bet. How about it?"

Why not? "Sure. I'll be done at the Embassy around five. Major Simpson kept us late all last week and he swore we'd be back to normal hours again."

"Where shall we meet?"

"How about outside the Embassy at 5:30?"

"Sounds good." He leaned closer. "May I?"

When she smiled, he kissed her cheek softly. "Until tomorrow."

* * *

74

CHAPTER 15

Why was Joe here so early? A glance at her watch told Phyllis it was 4:30, a full hour before they'd arranged to meet. She'd walked out of the Officers' Mess after a late cup of tea when she spotted him talking to several girls from the steno pool. What was he, a ladykiller?

She and Lorraine watched him for a few minutes, her frown morphing to a scowl just as he looked over. However upset she was at his untimely entrance, there was no mistaking the sexy smile he proudly donned at seeing her. All the girls turned to see who had stolen his attention; their expressions registered disappointment and resignation. Super. Another reason for them all to hate her. Thanks, Joe.

Lorraine rolled her eyes. "Good luck, sweetie. Don't do anything I wouldn't."

Laughing, Phyllis lightly punched her arm. "That gives me lots of room to maneuver."

Ignoring the man heading over, she and Lorraine parted ways at the staircase. She'd started up the steps when Joe bounded to her side.

"Hi Phyllis. How are you today?"

"You're early, Joe."

"I had some papers to deliver to your boss, so it's part business, part pleasure."

"How nice for you."

He fell in step with her. "You don't seem overjoyed to see me. We did have a supper date, right?"

Glancing back at the women still watching them, she shrugged. "Didn't know you were so popular at the Embassy."

"I'm not, but it's not my first time here either. I know a few gals in the pool."

She bet he did. "Maybe it's not a good day for me."

"Phyllis." He stopped her before they went into her office.

"What?"

"I'm on the level. No hidden agenda. I just wanted to take you to dinner, spend some time with you." He cupped her chin. "Is that so awful?"

His gaze locked with hers and she couldn't look away. Maybe he was a smoothie, but her gut said he was all right. Of course, it remained to be seen how correct her gut was.

"Phyllis!" Dickie's voice rang out. "I need you!"

She shrugged at Joe. "Duty calls."

"Introduce us, would you?"

She took him into Dickie's office, stood to one side when Joe marched to the front of his desk.

"Major Simpson, this is Joe Schneider from the State Department office off Grosvenor Square. He has some business with you, I believe."

Joe's hand shot out to pump Dickie's. "Nice to meet you, sir."

"Same. Have a seat and tell me what I can do for you." Dickie winked at Phyllis. "I assume you have business with her too."

Phyllis blushed and said with an irritated tone, "Excuse me, Major Simpson, but I have work to finish before leaving today."

"Sure, sure. Don't get mad at me, Miss Bowden." With an arched brow, he waved Joe into a chair. Phyllis hurried back to her desk with a small burn going.

She poked her typewriter keys with more force than necessary creating a few errors, so she had to start her letter over. Ripping out the paper, she balled it up and winged it forcefully into the trash bin like a major league pitcher.

The voices in Dickie's office weren't muted and Phyllis could hear them laughing, suddenly the best of friends. She strained to listen and was dying to hear one of them say the word 'salamander'. Dickie hadn't mentioned it again since the night she'd stayed so late. Maybe it meant something and maybe it didn't. She might have to force the play here to have any understanding at all.

Dinner that night was fun, uneventful. Joe charmed her out of her bad mood with refreshingly delightful conversation. If he was trying to sweep her off her feet, he was making a good start. They'd gotten into Rainbow Corner, the American club for GIs near Piccadilly Circus. Always crowded, the club was open twenty-four hours daily to provide recreation facilities, programs and food to American servicemen, but it also provided top-notch musical entertainment.

Bands. Glenn Miller and Artie Shaw had played there along with some colorful names like the Hepcats, The Flying Yanks and The Thunder Bolts. Everyone always had a great time at the club and Phyllis was enjoying the evening very much.

After jitterbugging through two songs, she begged for a coke to whet her whistle. She and Joe wended their way through the crowd to the long soda fountain where she was amazed to see they still had ice. No carbonation though, since the beverage began as syrup from a barrel, but that was all right. It was a little piece of home in the middle of war-torn London, brightening faces of the young servicemen for a brief period of time. Better brief than not at all.

"This is fabulous. We don't get soda at all anymore," said Phyllis sipping her coke. "London feels worn-out to me."

"Me too. I've been here six months and the devastation in some areas is horrifying. If Hitler was trying to break London, however, he sure missed the boat."

"True. Even with the long lines outside shops, boarded-up windows and everyday shabbiness, Londoners have shown they're not quitters but must be exhausted after five years of war."

"And the smell!"

She touched Joe's arm. "I know! Isn't it awful? I suppose you can get used to it, but I've been here over eight months and the pervasive smell is kinda like—"

"...Dust," he finished.

"I agree. It's so acrid you can taste it." Phyllis wrinkled her nose making Joe laugh. "I'll be back. I need to find the ladies' room."

He pointed toward the rear of the club. "It's that way. I'll be here, guarding your coke."

She smiled. "Please do. I'm not done with it yet."

In the restroom, she chatted briefly with a girl from the steno pool. The atmosphere at the Embassy had thawed somewhat enabling Phyllis to once again enjoy her work, and a bit of the camaraderie she'd known before. Threading her way through the crowd back to the soda fountain, her eyes fell on a short man in a gabardine trench coat, clutching a homburg speaking in Joe's ear.

Phyllis froze behind several GIs laughing and talking with a few women, but she still had a clear view. *Who was this guy?* And her question wasn't meant merely for Homburg Man, but for Joe Schneider too. She barely knew him. Did he actually work for the State Department? Lorraine vouched for him, but she was a pushover for a handsome man, a provable fact as personal experience had illustrated.

When the GIs and their girls wandered to the dance floor, Joe caught sight of her and waved. Her eyes narrowed as she waved back watching the short man walk past Joe and out the door. But she'd seen them talking, so he wouldn't be able to say he hadn't seen him. Joe smiled his lovely smile and lifted her glass in salute. By the time she reached him, she knew what she had to do.

"I saved your space and your coke, although some guy tried to steal it from me," he teased.

"Was it that short man in the homburg? I thought I saw him speak with you." She kept her expression blank even though Joe's cheerful demeanor never wavered.

"Oh yeah. That was Silas Reardon. Don't you know him?"

"Why would I?"

"He used to work at the American Embassy as undersecretary to William Bradley."

She kept her face neutral under Joe's scrutiny. He seemed to be testing her for some reason.

"Nope. Don't know him. That was before my time."

"True," he shrugged, sipped his coke, "it's just that he's at the Embassy sometimes doing consulting for some of the higher ups. Just thought you might have seen him."

Her lips tightened; it didn't seem like a good time to admit she had seen him at the Embassy talking to Dickie. In fact, she wasn't about to admit anything to a man she'd just met. *Trust no one.* Ann Fletcher's words came softly creeping into her conscious. *Say nothing.* Crap. Maybe she'd already said too much to Joe Schneider, debonair ladies man and obviously man-about-town. What had slipped out in her champagne haze at the party last night?

When the date wound down and Joe escorted her home, he took her hand leaving her at the doorstep.

"This was fun. I had a good time tonight." He really did have the nicest smile.

"I did too."

"In that case," his smile broadened, "could I see you again? There's a—"

"Wait a minute, Joe," she interrupted.

"What?"

"This is going a little fast for me."

"There's a war on, Phyllis, and who knows how long we'll be here. I mean that literally."

She nodded. "It's a good point, but how about this—leave me your number and I'll call you." When his eyebrows shot up in his hairline, she snickered. "I don't mean to be forward, but I've got a lot going on right now. I'll call when something fun comes up."

He fished a card out of his pocket. "Here's my number. Can I reciprocate though? If you call me, next time I call you."

She stared at the card. "We're getting ahead of ourselves."

"Okay, okay," he laughed. "I'll wait for your call, just don't take too long. There's a new band coming to the Savoy that I'd like to hear."

"The Savoy? I thought it was bombed."

"Of course it was, but it's been reopened for business."

"Let me think about it."

Joe kissed her cheek and watched her go in. Once safely inside, Phyllis leaned back against the solid door wondering. Why wasn't she more excited about this cute guy? Most wartime relationships were fast and generally just for fun. Why did she get the feeling there was more to this book than his attractive cover?

She had some thinking to do, and a plan to put into action. Better get on with it.

* * *

CHAPTER 16

Dickie's flashlight dropped out of his hand bouncing a spray of light against an enormous mound of rubble where an apartment building had been.

"Mind your torch!" came a quick rebuke from a bobby across the street. Dickie picked it up carefully making sure its beam was now aimed at the ground. The batteries were dying anyway and he had thought to install fresh ones before he lit out tonight, but the voice on the phone had been insistent. So he forgot the batteries. He had nearly forgotten his coat and hat too. Slamming down the phone, he'd dashed out his office with focused concentration. At the Embassy door, someone had yelled 'goodbye' to him, causing him to remember what he had forgotten. He ran back upstairs just as Phyllis came out of the supply closet down the hall. Stopping abruptly, he watched curiously as she opened and closed the door a few times.

"Won't it lock?"

She shook her head. "No. I guess it only locks when I'm in there."

Dickie wasn't sure whether to laugh or not. "Get maintenance to have a look tomorrow."

"Yes, sir. You off?"

"Just." Grabbing the coat and hat, he hurried through her office. "Good night."

"Have a good evening, sir."

"You too."

And he was out of the Embassy before either could say anything further. It was still blacker than black outside. London wasn't as dark as it had been during the Blitz, but few homes had removed blackout curtains. Cars and street lamps still had their darkened disguises, so the city crawled in these waning days of the war.

After the bobby's warning, Dickie's thoughts turned to his job. He'd had a good career in the Army and was still relatively young when promoted to Major, a source of pride. But he really couldn't understand why the President had appointed him to take over for Lt. Col. Lawrence. Although he couldn't think of a precedent when a military attaché had been accused of espionage, it seemed like the logical choice to replace Lawrence would have been with someone more experienced, someone from another Embassy. Certainly not an Army major with little diplomatic experience and his last billet in North Africa. His transfer to London had come out of the blue.

Walking past a bombed out brick building, Dickie saw several soot-covered children playing in the debris. His nose breathed in a pungent smell just as women's voices called out scattering the children. By the time he had walked by, everyone was gone leaving the darkened area ghostlike with rising dust.

Working with Phyllis Bowden was all right. She was skittish at first, but they'd managed to work out most of their initial difficulties and now he considered her a first-rate secretary. And he was grateful she continued with him when he moved into the Military Attache position because he knew some women wouldn't have wanted a position with that much spotlight. Phyllis took things in stride admirably and he felt they functioned well as a team.

Except lately.

She'd grown quiet in the last week or so, not like herself at all. This thing with Ronnie may have spooked her or maybe she had put in for a transfer. Sure there had been some late nights, tiresome but necessary, and the incident with the supply closet still nagged at him. He felt she was covering up some kind of problem. He shrugged it off; he had his own problems. Shadows loomed in the dark—Dickie picked up the pace.

He had been in the job for nearly two weeks now, but he knew he would never really fill Lawrence's shoes. Lt. Col. Lawrence was a career diplomat with a reputation as a man who got the job done. It was unthinkable that Lawrence was dishonest and a traitor to his country, but what did he know? The higher ups must know something that he didn't or Lawrence wouldn't be sitting in the brig right now.

Dickie gave a full body shudder. He was hoping to tread water until the war was over and then be transferred elsewhere. Norway might be nice. And he had questions about his new position, questions that normally would have been answered by the outgoing military attaché. Since Lawrence was in jail, he had nowhere to go.

Yeah, there were many things he didn't understand.

Like tonight.

His feet were taking him closer to a small pub several streets over from the Embassy. He wasn't sure where it was and almost missed the doorway when he suddenly came upon it. A tattered awning hung over several small windowpanes with blackout tape. Squinting, he could barely make out the words *Nicholson's* on the shredded cloth and knew it was the right destination. Parts of the door had been blown away and patched, but the ruined look of the pub never gave him pause. Most of London looked like this after five long years of war with Germany.

Inside the pub was nearly as dim as outside. Smoke hung in the stale air. A worn-out bar on one side of a smallish room stood in front of a once ornate mirror, now mere shards with bits of silver color. A few bottles of whiskey waited patiently on a low shelf while a skinny man with a tattoo on his arm filled thick glasses of ale from a nearby keg. Two tired-looking patrons on rickety bar stools reached for their beers as Dickie's eyes swept the room. A man in a gabardine trench coat sat towards the back of the dingy pub. He raised a hand when Dickie spotted him and wandered over.

"Look. What's this about, Silas? And what's with all the cloak and dagger?" He plopped in a chair, glaring at the stout man across the table. "Some guy calls, mentions a salamander account, like I know what that is, and tells me to come here."

"That was just code for us to meet."

"This is ridiculous. I already know you."

"I have information about Lawrence."

Dickie blinked unbelieving eyes. "What kind of information? Something to help clear him? And why should I trust you?"

"You shouldn't, that's true, but I'm here to make a deal with you." Silas pushed a glass of beer towards Dickie who stared at it, eyes narrowing.

"Go ahead. It's not poisoned."

Dickie picked it up and gulped a quarter of the frothy liquid before setting it down. He licked his lips.

"What kind of deal?"

"You help me and I help you. It's that simple."

"Nothing is that simple."

"If I have to, Simpson," he began with a clipped, harsh tone, "I'll spread the word about what happened in North Africa." Dickie nearly knocked over his glass in his haste to push back from the table.

"Nothing…"

"Don't even think of lying to me." His hard tone softened. "But none of that needs to come out if you'll just do a small favor for me."

Dickie stared at Silas saying nothing, but burned a hole in those beady eyes.

"Here's all you have do…"

* * *

84

CHAPTER 17

"Why is that so funny?"

"I'm not sure," giggled Lorraine. "Maybe it's because I had a whiskey instead of the usual beer."

"You had two whiskies."

"I stand corrected."

"Where's Joe tonight?"

Phyllis glared at her. "We're not attached at the hip."

"Okay, okay. Calm down. I thought you liked him."

"You see several guys at a time, why can't I?"

Lorraine laughed, took another sip shivering as it went down. "Mmm... good stuff. Anyway," she wiped her mouth, "You take 'em one at a time, Phyl, and you know you do."

She shrugged, pulled her coat around her. "I'm chilly. Why don't we go home?"

"I know what you need." Lorraine held up two fingers to Mick behind the bar at Angel's. The burly owner came right away to plunk down two more whiskies in front of the girls. "Thanks, Mick." He smiled his crooked smile and lumbered off to the bar.

"I'm not that thirsty tonight, Lorraine."

She raised the glass to Phyllis' lips. "Here. It's good for you. It'll certainly warm up your insides."

Lorraine was probably right, so Phyllis reached for the glass and took a small sip. She mimicked Lorraine's full-body shiver as the liquor worked its way down her throat, scorching as it went. Her eyes widened and she coughed.

"Oh! Check to see if you brought any cigarettes tonight. I know I don't have any." She nudged Phyllis. "Have to visit the ladies' room. Be right back."

Phyllis opened her leather purse to rummage through the contents. Pushing past her lipstick tube, comb and wallet, she couldn't find any cigarettes either. A woman from the steno pool at the Embassy bumped her, said hello and they spoke for a few minutes. When Phyllis went back to checking her purse, she peered into a side compartment rarely used. Something white caught her eye. Pulling it out, it was just a small slip of paper, but opening it made her gasp.

Lots of numbers in two rows were printed legibly with black ink. It looked like the kind of ink they used at the Embassy and she knew that brand was hard to get in wartime. It was just a seemingly random series of numbers making her wonder if they meant anything. When nothing came to mind, she concentrated instead on how the paper might have gotten in her purse. It certainly wasn't a receipt. *Look for anything unusual.* A piece of paper with black numbers was very unusual and a fragment of memory fluttered in her mind.

Phyllis was taking notes at a meeting with Ronald Lawrence, Dick Simpson and two other Army staffers. When was this? Maybe three months ago when Amy was out sick and she'd filled in for her.

Anyway, the meeting was going as usual in the large corner conference room upstairs at the Embassy. She remembered squinting from the sunshine reflecting off her white pad and Dickie had gotten up to lower the shade for her. Ronnie was in good spirits that day and had even cracked a small joke about Army life. Everyone had laughed, it was one they'd all heard, but the atmosphere was light and she felt good being part of a team. When the men stood to leave, she'd openly admired their smart uniforms, straight postures, and clean-shaven faces. They were good men and she was proud of her work, proud to be a cog in this important wheel bringing an end to the war.

Phyllis went back to her desk to type up the minutes from the meeting. Ronnie had walked back with Dick Simpson for further conversation in Dickie's office when Ronnie stopped by her desk. He asked Dickie to go ahead and he'd be there in a minute.

"You're working too hard, Phyllis. You should take a little time off. Go up to Scotland with friends."

"I don't know when I'd have time to do that, sir, much less the money."

"The war seems to be shortening our lives. Have fun however you can. Here…" Lawrence reached into his pocket for some money. He thrust a twenty at her. "At least let me treat you and Lorraine to lunch today. Go over to Harrod's and take a long lunch."

"Oh, no, sir! I couldn't take your money."

"Then do it for Lorraine," he smirked. "I know she'll take it."

"Well, I…"

"No refusals, Miss Bowden. I absolutely insist."

"Okay, if I have no choice."

Phyllis reached into a drawer for her purse and then the strangest thing happened: Ronnie stumbled somehow, knocking the purse out of her hands. Contents fell all over the floor around her chair.

"Oh, I'm so sorry! Let me get that for you."

He picked up her comb, lipstick and other things that had fallen out and tucked them neatly back in for her. She watched amazed at his thoughtfulness. After zipping the purse closed, he handed it back.

"Sorry about that."

"That's okay."

"You never know when you're going to need it."

"Need what, sir?"

Ronald Lawrence just smiled and walked away into Dickie's office. She was still confused when he came out an hour later, smiled again and returned to his office upstairs.

Had Lt. Col. Lawrence, the Military Attache of the American Embassy, slipped that piece of paper in her purse?

Lorraine was standing by the table. "Hey!" She snapped her fingers in Phyllis' face. "Where'd you go?"

Phyllis continued staring at the paper in her hand.

"You're seriously spaced out. What gives?" Sitting down at the table, Lorraine reached over to pluck the paper from Phyllis. "What's this?"

Taking a deep breath, Phyllis said in a low voice, "What would you say if I told you it could be a coded message?"

Lorraine laughed out loud, but her laughter faded when she focused on Phyllis' solemn face.

"You're not kidding."

"No."

"You think these numbers are some sort of code?"

"I don't know. It's a possibility."

"Why is it a possibility?"

"Lorraine," she leaned closer, "I'm pretty sure Ronnie put that paper in my purse a few months ago."

"Ronnie did?"

"Yeah, I was just remembering when it happened."

"Maybe that's the when, but what's the *why?*"

Phyllis shook her head. "I have no answers for you."

They both continued to stare at the paper in Lorraine's hand until she shivered and handed it back to Phyllis. "Here, you take it. Gives me the heebie-jeebies."

"I think Ronnie knew he was in trouble."

"Why in the world would he put something like that in your purse? What is it? A clue?"

"Maybe."

Lorraine chuckled, took a last sip of her whiskey. "Well, you're no Sherlock Holmes."

Phyllis' eyes slid her way. "I think Ronnie nominated me to become Sherlock."

"Why you?"

"Amy said he complimented me one time on my inventiveness."

"So you're supposed to invent him out of jail?" She couldn't hide her smirk.

Phyllis tucked the paper back in her purse. "I need help, Lorraine. You know most of the guys in London. Who could help me—"

"—Decipher an encrypted message?"

"That's right," Phyllis smiled. "Reach into your little black book and pull out a name for me."

Lorraine held up a finger to Mick who promptly brought her another whiskey. She sipped, shrugged and laid a finger alongside her nose. "I may know somebody."

"Aha. Who, pray tell?"

"I do know this man who works in encryption in the basement of the State Department."

"I'm not even going to ask how you met a man who works in a basement."

Lorraine patted her hair. "Don't. It's a boring story compared to some of the others."

Phyllis laughed. "Just tell me already."

"His name is Willie Winter."

"You're kidding."

"No, that's his name. Honestly."

"No parent in their right mind would name a kid William Winter."

"Oh, I don't know." Lorraine waved a hand in the air. "It has a certain ring to it."

"Does he work for the British or for us?"

"Both, I think. Want to meet him?"

"Yes, please and as soon as possible."

"That can be arranged if you're sure. Tread lightly, my friend. You could be stepping on someone's toes."

"I will."

But treading lightly was much harder than she imagined it would be.

* * *

CHAPTER 18

Wise Willie Winter read the colorful sign on the door in this subterranean dungeon. Phyllis had walked down two flights of stairs from offices above to a dank, dark place where only mushrooms could grow. The stone walls she'd passed were glistening with moisture and the whole place was this side of creepy. And there was this unidentifiable smell that made her nose crinkle. But Willie's bright yellow sign had bold, red letters that must have been someone's idea of a joke.

Phyllis wasn't laughing as she knocked softly before entering.

"Come in," a muffled voice called out.

A thin man with black glasses and pointy hair sitting at a large desk amidst volumes of paper looked up from his work as she walked in. He kept a steady gaze on her until she stood right in front of him.

"Willie Winter?"

"Who's asking?"

"I'm Phyllis Bowden. My friend Lorraine Watkins called you and confirmed this meeting."

"Yeah, I got it." He tilted his head towards a chair. "Have a seat. If you didn't have an appointment, they wouldn't have let you in upstairs."

She glanced at his messy desk. "I'm surprised you agreed to see me. Your work looks classified."

"It is," he acknowledged, "but Lorraine can be, shall we say, very persuasive." That earned him a smile.

"She can be that."

"Besides you have a G2 security clearance or else we wouldn't be speaking at all. So, Miss Bowden, what can I do for you?"

She fished the paper from her purse. "I found this recently and I think it may be a coded message. Can you look at it and tell me what it means?" She reached across the desk to hand it to him. Staring at it, his eyes began to widen with interest.

"This is a code we haven't used for a while because the Germans caught on to it." Willie glanced over. "Where'd you get this?"

"I found it in my purse."

"How did it get there?"

"I'm not sure. Someone may have put it there without my knowledge."

"No kiddin'? Recently?"

"No, a few months ago. I just discovered it last night."

He was quiet for a moment, then opened a bottom drawer to take out a small book. Skimming through pages, he stopped and placed his finger on a certain paragraph. He moved his finger down the lines until he found what he was looking for. His gaze transferred back to her little scrap of paper and he suddenly went into action.

Willie shuffled through the mess on his desk for a pad of lined paper and a stubby pencil. Shifting his eyes between Phyllis' note and the book, he began to write words on the pad. After scribbling noisily for a few minutes, he looked up. "Sure you don't know what this says?"

"I'm sure."

"It's a list of equipment."

"Equipment?" Phyllis scooted to the front of her chair. "Like tables and chairs?"

"More like tanks and guns." He leveled a steely look her way. "You shouldn't be walking around with this in your purse. It might fall in the wrong hands."

"I didn't know what it was."

"This is classified information, way out of your pay grade. Mine too for that matter but I'm closer than you are."

She threw out her hands defensively. "I swear I didn't know what it was."

Willie rose quickly knocking his chair over. "I need to report this to my commanding officer."

"No, I…"

He hurried around the desk and made his way to the door before she could stop him.

"Wait a minute!"

"Can't wait." She caught one end of his white shirt he hadn't bothered to tuck in and tugged for him to stop. "Hey, let go."

Rushing from the room, Willie hurried down a long hallway and up the back stairs with Phyllis hot on his heels. She was getting panicky when he tripped on an untied shoelace and tumbled to the floor. Phyllis helped him up and shoved him into a nearby janitor's closet.

"Give me a minute. Talk to me."

He poised his foot on a bucket to retie the lace. "Can't. You shouldn't have this information."

"And I don't want it, but can you at least give me a hint about it?"

His withering look unnerved her. "Phyllis, I don't want to lose my job."

"Please…just a hint."

After finishing with his shoe, he stared at her for a long moment. "This goes nowhere, right?"

"Right."

"It looks like a list of equipment that may be left after the war is over."

"Why would someone want to know that?"

He handed the paper to her. "I have a few ideas that I shouldn't. Burn this and I'll forget I ever saw you."

"Done."

Willie peeked out the door, looked both ways and scurried back to his dungeon. Phyllis stuffed the paper back into her purse, wondering where she could stow it for safekeeping. When she left the closet, Willie was long gone and she headed home.

Burn it! That's what Dickie did that night. The message had to be top secret, so why would Ronnie Lawrence hide it in her purse?

She needed more information and fast.

* * *

CHAPTER 19

"So you broke down and called him?"

"Ah...yes, I did."

"Why?" Lorraine asked. "I thought you weren't going to see him again."

"I changed my mind."

"Phyllis—"

Lorraine had backed her up until her butt bumped into the kitchen table. "Tell me what's going on."

"Hey! You guys fighting?" Mildred and Doris peeked around the corner clearly staying out of the line of fire.

Phyllis laughed and pushed Lorraine. "No. We're having a friendly discussion."

Doris' eyebrows shot up. "Doesn't look friendly but we'll leave you to it." The doorbell rang, piercing the air. "I'll get it!"

Lorraine poked her finger in Phyllis' chest. "That's for you, isn't it?"

"Jealous?"

She didn't crack a smile. "When you get home tonight, I want a full report on what you're up to."

"Who says I'm up to anything?"

"Stop with the innocent face. I know you. Just talk to me, okay?"

Phyllis slipped past her, turned at the doorway. "I will want to talk to you tonight, so stay up." Lorraine nodded and she headed for the front door. "Curtain up," Phyllis whispered before she rounded a corner and met Joe with a smile.

The Savoy Hotel was swoon-worthy.

Joe looked so handsome in his grey flannel suit, white dress shirt and deep red tie that Phyllis was tempted to take a bite out of him. She took ahold of his arm instead.

The Savoy was such an iconic place from inception, as Joe had been telling her on the way over in the taxi. She quit ogling the elegant entrance to the luxury hotel and tuned in to what he was saying.

"...So it burned down in the Peasant's Revolt when it was the home of John of Gaunt, King Richard II's uncle."

"When was this?"

"In 1381. The peasants were upset about the poll tax and refused to pay it."

She glanced at his neatly combed black hair, angular jawline and smooth cheeks trying not to sigh. "I guess this was a big deal in history."

"It was indeed," he smiled. "The peasants were treated better after that and it began the breakdown of the feudal system."

Walking into the lobby, Phyllis' eyes widened. "Well, it sure has changed since all those years ago. I assume they rebuilt it."

"Many times."

She marveled at the high, decorative ceilings, Roman columns with black and white checked tile floor and uniformed footmen ready to serve. She openly gawked at the numerous crystal chandeliers hanging overhead brightly illuminating the gorgeous interior.

"It's changed more than you know, Phyllis." Joe lowered his voice. "You must have heard that rich Londoners thumbed their noses at Hitler here with their pink gin and blackout balls."

She laughed. "I've heard. I've never experienced the phenomenon firsthand though." Glancing around, she asked, "Where are we going?"

"To a dance in one of the ballrooms." He stopped to put his lips close to her ear. His whispery voice made her stomach flutter. "They say journalists file articles from makeshift offices in rooms here and spies use quiet suites for debriefings and interrogations."

Phyllis blinked at him. Why was he telling her this? "I guess you boys at the State Department know more than we do at the American Embassy."

His nice smile faded when he brought her hand to his full lips for a kiss; she had to lock her knees to keep from wobbling. *Focus!*

Music could be heard all over the elegant hotel but the volume increased as Joe and Phyllis made their way to a richly decorated ballroom. She'd never seen anything like it. The enormous cavern of a room had a rounded ceiling covered with colorful mosaic tiles. Bright lights dangled from above and along the walls giving just the right amount of light for dancers to be able to see their partners and those around them. On a raised platform towards the front, a tuxedoed band played such lively music everyone was on their feet, moving to the beat. Phyllis couldn't tell pauper from aristocrat as her anxious eyes roamed the crowded ballroom. It wasn't what she expected but she was glad of that—she was concerned she hadn't worn the right clothes when he suggested they come here tonight. But her red silk wiggle dress with her newest peep toe heels fit in perfectly and she quietly breathed a sigh of relief.

"Let's dance!" he shouted above the din. When she nodded, Joe grabbed her hand and led her into the middle of the gyrating crowd. Several hours flew by as they would dance a few numbers and sit one out, taking a breather and drinking the delicious pink gin. It was served straight up with a lemon garnish and tickled Phyllis' nose as she sipped. When the band took breaks, they talked about their work and lives to the point where Phyllis began to wonder if she was wrong about him. The classy man in the great suit who moved his chair close to her and looked at no other girl in the room seemed sweet and genuine. Sincere and truthful. Maybe he was on the level like he'd told her in the beginning.

And then again she didn't know him that well, but maybe she wanted to after all. With conflicted feelings, Phyllis didn't stop him when he brushed his lips against hers during a slow number. When she didn't object, he kissed her again and then again, more deeply each time. She felt herself melting into him and her insides liquefying in his arms. Her plan of trying to figure out what he knew was fading away and she couldn't have cared less. When he tugged her away from the crowd into a darkened corner, Joe cupped her chin to keep her eyes on his.

His hand slid to the nape of her neck to slowly draw her body closer. She tore her eyes away to focus on his tempting lips just a breath away. When his lips descended, Phyllis knew she was done for and kissed him like there was no tomorrow. In wartime, it just might be. He moved her deeper into the corner never removing his lips from hers. She sighed against his mouth as he angled his head to deliver insistent kisses that lit her on fire with desire she'd never known and turned her brain into gelatinous mush. With a room full of energetic souls and loud music, Joe wove a spell around Phyllis that cocooned them both in a loving embrace.

All too soon it was the wee hours of the morning and the band called it quits. Partiers still partied on, but Joe took Phyllis home, carefully tucking her close in the taxi. At the door his determined mouth took hers again for another spine-melting, angels-weeping kiss to end all kisses. She thought she heard him say he'd call her tomorrow as she floated into the house and up the stairs to her room. Soft yet persistent knocking finally brought Phyllis back down to earth and she opened her door.

"What?"

"What do you mean 'what'? We were going to talk."

It was hard to focus on Lorraine's inquiring face, but Phyllis finally blinked rapidly, shaking her head.

"What about?"

"You told me you wanted to talk tonight no matter when you got in." Lorraine's dark eyes narrowed. Her head tilted to one side assessing her friend's face. "You've been kissing."

Phyllis backed up, hands in front. "No way."

"Yes, ma'am." She touched Phyllis' lips. "Your lips are all puffy. I know kissing and you've been kissing Joe." She stood in the middle of the room with her hands on her hips. "What gives? You like this guy? I didn't think you trusted him. Have you flipped your wig?"

Phyllis grabbed Lorraine's hand and dragged her to the bed. "Shh! Do you want to tell all the girls in the house? Mrs. Stewart too?"

"If you kissed him goodnight on the doorstep, trust me. Mrs. Stewart already knows. She's got radar."

"Fine. Listen. We do need to talk."

Lorraine chuckled. "Have your wits about you now?" Smiling, she held up two fingers. "Can you focus? How many fingers am I holding up?"

"Oh, ha." Phyllis frowned. "Like you've never kissed a man before. Is it a crime if I do?"

"No, honey." Lorraine bit back a smirk. "I think you're gathering information about Joe...trying to see if you can trust him. Am I getting warm?"

"You are. I'm going to need someone like him to help me." Phyllis sank to the bed beside her. "And I can separate my emotions from my intellect, thank you, but he still bears watching," she pointed a finger at Lorraine, "so this is what I want you to do..."

* * *

CHAPTER 20

Lorraine sweet-talked her 'guy of the moment' into doing Phyllis' bidding. She'd had a beef with Henry so he was off her list…for the present. It depended on how accommodating he was in the future whether he returned to her list or not.

Lorraine had her standards. As youngest of three daughters, she knew how to get her way after years of practice with her long-suffering daddy from Kentucky. Her soft voice had a hint of southern spice smoothing any request from the beautiful blonde. Not many men were immune to her feminine wiles. She had been able to charm Roger Eden, an RAF flier they all knew and shared occasionally, for the evening on the pretense of running a small errand for her. He was in town but currently without a female companion since Norma needed to wash her hair and Mildred and Doris had duty in a local convalescent home. The gangly Brit was lonely and more than happy to do what Lorraine asked as a favor to all the pretty girls at Seven Addison Bridge Place.

That settled, Lorraine got down to brass tacks explaining what she needed Roger to do. With Phyllis working late that night and the rest of her roommates busy, Lorraine headed down alone to the Blue Anchor after Roger's phone call a couple of hours later. When she walked into the gritty pub, another window had been shattered from the latest buzz bomb, leaving few in one piece, but Malcolm was as cheery as ever. It was hard to be down when the ale was flowing. The full bearded Scot brightened when she walked in the pub. He wandered over to pull out her chair.

"Why, thank you, Malcolm," she gushed, "aren't you the gentleman?"

"Aye, lassie, that I am." His dark eyes fairly gleamed taking her all in with a sweeping look. "Lookin' bonny tonight, you are. Are ye expectin' company?" His ardent expression said he hoped she wasn't.

Lorraine took out a comb to smooth her sunny hair. "Are all you Scots so sweet or is it just you, Malcolm?" She tucked the comb in her purse. "Because you know what happened last time we met up." The sparkle in his eye told her he remembered all right. She snorted—bloody Scots didn't date; they just took you to bed and you'd be lucky if you ever saw them again. Dating wasn't in their repertoire, so his continued advances sweetened the pot for her.

"I think you've gotten all you're going to get from Lorraine Watkins."

"Now honey…"

"Don't 'now honey' me." She raised a brow playfully. "Charm another lucky lady tonight because I'm meeting someone." Disappointment flooded his face. "And here he comes, so would you please bring us two whiskies." When she patted Malcolm's beefy arm, he reluctantly headed back to the crowded bar.

She waved at Roger coming in the door. "Yoo hoo! Over here, Rog." The tall Brit wove a path through thirsty patrons to her table towards the back. He smiled when he saw her, pushing aside the thick brown hair that always flopped in his face.

Malcolm delivered the whiskies just as Roger sat down. With a scowl, he put them on the table and left.

"What's with him?" asked Roger.

"Don't worry about Malcolm. His expectations for the evening just fell flat."

"Huh?"

"Never mind. Let's talk about what happened tonight." Lorraine raised her glass. "And here's to handsome fliers."

He raised his glass to meet hers. "Handsome fliers who are winning the war." The corners of his lips quirked up.

"God save the King."

"God save the King."

They tossed back the brown liquid, coughed and wiped their mouths. Lorraine did another full body shudder leaving Roger with a wide grin on his youthful face. He had that smooth, pale complexion that was common to the English probably from all the tea they drank, Lorraine guessed. Or maybe it was genes…anyway…

"So? How did it go?"

He gave her a strange look. "Maybe not so good. I guess it all depends on your point of view."

"Just tell me everything you saw, Rog, and I'll take it from there."

"All right." Pushing at that hunk of hair again, he took a deep breath. "I waited at a café across from the State Department building and had a cupper while waitin'. I wasn't there more than an hour when the bloke came out and started walking down the street."

"What time was this?"

"Probably six." He gave her the once-over. "You know you really never said why you wanted me to follow him. If he and I hadn't met at one of you girls' parties, I wouldn't have known what he looks like to help you."

She purred and patted his arm. "And I'm ever so grateful that you were able to help me." *Maybe distraction will help.* "Who is it again you want me to get you a date with?"

"Norma please," he sighed. "I'm a sucker for a gorgeous redhead."

"She is that. Can you continue?"

"Sure, sure. Where was I?" *Yes, distraction works.*

"He started walking down the street."

"Right. Well, I followed him down to the train station at Bond Street. I almost lost him several times, what with it being Friday night and all the GIs were heading back to base or wherever."

"It was crowded?"

"Massively. Like I said, I nearly lost the bloke a few times but I kept with him pretty well. He's tall, which helped me to see him with all the people around."

"So he went into the train station at Bond Street?" Roger nodded. "Did he get on a train?"

"That's what I assumed he would do, but he didn't. He was meeting someone, not going anywhere."

"Who did he meet?"

Roger lowered his head. "Is he seein' one of your roommates?"

"Yes."

"That's what I was afraid of." He looked sheepish. "Norma?"

"No, Phyllis. Why?"

He took ahold of her hand. "Because a train came in and a woman got off. They hugged and he kissed her."

Lorraine was quiet. "Where did he kiss her?"

"On the train platform."

She laughed. "No, where on her face?"

"On the cheek."

"Okay. Then what?"

"They spoke for a few minutes, then she passed something to him, I couldn't see what, and she got back on the train and left."

Her lips parted in surprise. "She just got back on and left?"

"Yeah. Surprised me too. I thought he was pickin' up a girlfriend or something. Maybe she was his sister."

"So they didn't look intimate?"

He scrunched his nose. "How would they do that?"

"Oh, come on, Rog," she scolded. "You know what it looks like when a man and woman are intimate. They stand close together, whisper in each other's ears, kiss...like that."

"Well, they kissed, like I said, but it didn't seem intimate."

"Hmm. I'll have to find out if he has a sister." She held up two fingers to Malcolm.

"Maybe it was an old girlfriend and they had broken up or something."

"…Or something."

A grumpy Malcolm glared at Roger when he plunked down two more whiskies. "You havin' any food tonight, lassie?"

She shook her head. "Not tonight, Malcolm. I've got to take off." She handed him some money. "Will this cover the tab?"

His eyes widened and he jerked his thumb at Roger. "This fella ain't payin'?"

"No. He did me a favor and I told him I'd buy him a drink."

Malcolm wandered off mumbling under his breath about the *cheap bastard Lorraine was with.*

Roger smirked, downed his whiskey. "Nice guy. Friend of yours?"

"Sometimes." She downed her whiskey, coughed and stood. "I need to go. I'll talk to Norma about tomorrow night for you. How's that?"

"Perfect and I'm sorry I didn't have better news for you." He left a cigarette on the table and stood with her.

"I'm not sure if the news is good or bad, to be honest, Rog, but thanks for doing it."

"See you tomorrow night when I pick up my sweetie."

"See you then."

They parted ways at the doorway and walked off in different directions. She could hear his boots clicking on the dirty sidewalk, the sound becoming dimmer the farther away he walked. When she couldn't hear him at all, Lorraine turned the corner and headed home wondering what in the world she would say to her best friend whose new boyfriend, Joe, was just seen meeting another woman.

What was he doing with her?

Was he cheating on Phyllis?

Why had he wanted to meet Phyllis so badly if he was involved with somebody else?

It didn't look good, whatever the scene was about, and Lorraine dreaded telling her friend the results of her little scheme. A scheme that had surely backfired.

* * *

CHAPTER 21

So he was just using her? If that was his game, Joe Schneider, he of the incredible kisses, had another think coming. If Phyllis thought she was conflicted before, that was nothing compared to how she felt now.

After departing the tube by Covent Gardens, she kept her head low walking briskly down Shelton Street towards Ann Fletcher's flat. With only Lorraine to talk to, Phyllis was beginning to lose the bigger picture and her role in it.

Lorraine.

Her brows furrowed as she remembered Roger's report about Joe meeting some woman at the train station. It rubbed her raw. Emotions crashed and burned through her tumultuous brain. After the other night at the Savoy, Phyllis had begun to think that maybe Joe loved her.

Loved her? Ha! That'll be the day.

She was too easily swayed by a couple of smooches that obviously meant nothing to him and if that were the case? They would mean nothing to her. Case closed. Glancing around, she sought to clear her mind of Joe and think about what she was trying to do.

She slowed down her pace to stroll along the brick walkways finding Covent Gardens to be a respite from her usual workday at the Embassy where intrigue seemed to grow and fester. She practically wore tension like an overcoat, so coming here served two purposes: help and relaxation. People passed by laughing and talking, snacking, shopping or stopping for a meal at any number of restaurants and cafes that beckoned. GIs wandered spending money she knew the British desperately needed. Wishing she lived around here, Phyllis stopped to wistfully gaze at the piled plates of baked goods in the window of Gardens Boulangerie. Even in wartime, the shop was filled with homemade artisan breads, pastries and sandwiches luring her in like a bee to flowers.

She relented, said to hell with her diet and bought a chocolate raspberry-filled cake to take to Ann's. The aromas of lemon, caramel, chocolate and fresh-baked bread stimulated every olfactory nerve in her body, making her brain give out the order to do a little dance. Just in time, Phyllis caught her feet before they embarrassed her and she thanked the baker before leaving.

Another two stores down was the bookstore that Ann lived above. Her footsteps echoed as she suddenly looked around to see the crowd had thinned. Maybe she'd been in the bakery longer than she thought. With little warning, just a burp of air, Phyllis was thrown against the side of a building as a blast blew out the window of a small clothing store nearby. *Another damn bomb!* As she picked herself up off the sidewalk feeling aches and pains everywhere, she noticed the goodies in the bakery had been blown off their plates and more mannequins littered the street. She couldn't seem to get away from this grisly scene—and this war!

With muted sound echoing in her ears, she looked down to see her silk stockings shredded and legs coated with chocolate cake, her worn trench coat in tatters and one shoe missing. She brushed off the cake as best she could, sugary frosting clinging to her fingers, and daintily reached over to pick up her shoe wedged in the rubble. Slipping it back on was difficult since the shoe was a bit misshapen now and didn't fit properly. It was better than having no shoes at all. Her purse lay on its side, the strap missing. People were in quick time motion, dashing about trying to help the wounded wherever they lay. No one was killed, luckily, and the bomb appeared to have landed across the street with its concussive wave of sound causing the damage to stores on both sides. It was either a fluke or fate that this particular store on the whole street was chosen for destruction.

Phyllis scurried past the mess and went farther down to climb the stairs leading to Ann's upstairs flat. Her shaky hand only knocked once before the door was flung open and Ann grabbed her for a tight hug.

"Phyllis! I was so worried!"

Ann pulled her into the flat and wrapped her arms around her again. Phyllis' short puffs of air eventually became calmer and longer.

"Hitler almost got me that time, Ann," she whispered.

Ann patted her face. "Thank God he missed." She looked her over. "You need to clean up. Please use my loo. It's the first door down the hallway."

When Phyllis returned with her washed face looking a bit better, Ann towed her to a threadbare chair in the living room and pushed her gently into it. "Sit. Relax. I'll make you a cup of tea."

Phyllis suddenly realized her hands were empty. "Oh, Ann!"

"What?" Ann dashed back in, a box of tea in her hands. "Are you all right?"

"Yes, but…" Her fingers wiped the moisture from her cheeks.

"But what, dear?" Ann's tone reflected concern.

"I just bought a cake at the bakery downstairs before the bomb blast and it ended up all over me and the side of the building!"

"Oh…that would have been wonderful! I haven't had any spare money to buy such a treat."

Phyllis burst into tears.

Ann handed her a hanky. "Don't cry. It's all right." After Phyllis blew her nose, Ann went back into the kitchen to finish the tea. "I still have a few biscuits from the last time you were over. That will have to hold us."

She came back in holding a small tray with teapot, cups and saucers. A delicate silver package rested next to the pot. Phyllis rose to peel off her tattered trench coat. Dropping it on the floor, she remarked, "Do you have anything I could borrow to wear home? I'll make sure you get it back."

"Sure, sure. Don't worry about trivialities, dear. Just sit back down and enjoy your tea." Ann poured her a cup.

"Thanks. It's interesting how much I've gotten to like tea living in London."

Ann smiled, sat across from her and poured another cup. "I prefer tea to coffee now. Do you?"

"Since I can't get coffee very often, tea is just fine." Phyllis dropped a cube of sugar in her cup and stirred. Taking a sip, she nodded her head. "Darjeeling?"

"I stocked up before London starting running out of supplies. I may starve, but at least I'll have tea to drink."

Phyllis chuckled. "You really seem more English now than American."

"Oh, no. I'll always be true to my country, but I love England so much I wanted to stay."

"How long do you plan to remain?"

"I may return to the States after the war. I need to see my family."

"Is Mr. Bradley on your list of people to visit?"

Ann frowned, put her cup on a side table. "Speaking of Embassy personnel, you said on the phone you had some things to discuss with me. Are you composed enough for that conversation?"

Phyllis picked up a biscuit, chewed thoughtfully. After swallowing, she had another sip of tea before looking back at Ann waiting patiently. "I think so."

She settled back in her chair. "Let's hear it."

So Phyllis talked about Ann's hanky with the initials SR leading to the mysterious Silas Reardon. She went on about the ominous note in her purse and talking to an alarmed Willie Winter. When she talked about meeting Joe, Ann held up a hand.

"I didn't start all this, did I?"

"No, ma'am. Amy Broadbent did when she tried to kill herself over Ronnie's arrest."

"Oh, yes. Poor Amy Broadbent." Ann tsk-tsked into her cup.

"I have to ask you something, Ann."

"That doesn't mean I know the answer."

"Fine, but why did you steer me towards Silas? If the paper Ronnie slipped me…"

"That you *think* he slipped you," Ann corrected.

Phyllis nodded. "Okay, I think he slipped it to me, but if it's genuine and the message is about equipment that will be left after the war, where do I go from here? I can't find Silas Reardon anywhere in the vicinity."

Ann rose, plucked the teapot from the tray and walked into the kitchen to refill it. It took several minutes indicating to Phyllis that Ann was stalling, trying to figure out what to say—if anything. When at last she came back in to refill Phyllis' cup, Ann sat uneasily in her chair. Phyllis studied her as she tried to get comfortable, letting her take her time before she spoke. Ann was still the epitome of an English matron with dark hair and eyes, no-nonsense white blouse tucked into a sturdy wool skirt and sensible shoes. She didn't wear a bit of makeup but still looked youthful with her peachy complexion. At that moment Phyllis realized how shabby she must look with her bomb-blasted clothing and ill-fitting shoes. Irritated, she shook her head and ate the rest of her biscuit.

"Taste good?"

"Very nice."

"Thank you for bringing them."

"Are you dismissing me, Ann?"

"No, but I'm afraid what will happen to you if I do say something, anything. You're vulnerable, anxious and trouble has begun to follow you."

"I'll take my chances."

"This is bigger than all of us, Phyllis."

"So you know what's going on."

Ann cleared her throat. "I know bits and pieces. The big picture eludes me."

"I'm going to finish this, Ann, whether you help me or not."

"That's what I'm afraid of."

Phyllis stood, gathered her torn coat and purse, made to leave.

"Sit down, dear. I need to tell you something."

When Phyllis was sitting again, Ann sucked in a breath. "You need to watch your step. There are some very unscrupulous people where you work who have no compunction about hurting others. You could be next."

"How does Silas Reardon figure in this?"

"He's in the middle. I know Mr. Lawrence didn't trust him. Towards the end, he quit seeing Reardon completely and told me to refuse his phone calls."

"What did that mean?"

"Ronnie didn't say but after Reardon called the last time, I've never seen him so angry."

"Do you know what about?"

"No. Ronnie told me not to be involved with anything about Reardon, so I figured he was the culprit in whatever was going down."

"So it wasn't a surprise to you when Ronnie was arrested?"

"Of course, it was." Ann's eyes widened with alarm. "I thought for sure Reardon would be the one arrested."

"Arrested for what?"

"I think maybe that's what you stumbled upon with that note."

"You mean about equipment left over after the war? For the life of me I can't figure that one out."

Ann smiled, picked up her cup. "It makes sense if you think about it."

"I know nothing about tanks and guns, Ann."

"Maybe that's why Ronnie chose you."

"Chose me for what?"

"Someone out of the line of fire who could quietly learn the truth."

As cryptic as Ann was being, Phyllis thought she was probably on to something.

"And Joe Schneider?"

"Don't know him, but I'd tread carefully if I were you. Not knowing who to trust can be a dangerous business."

Phyllis leveled a cool look at her. "The only people I've trusted so far are Lorraine and you. I know Lorraine through and through and I know she's on my side. How about you, Ann Fletcher? Are you on my side or will I end up in a cell next to Lt. Col. Lawrence?"

Ann's eyes hardened. "I hate that you had to ask, yet I applaud you for having the guts to do so. Yes, I'm on your side, but I'm just a civilian now and have to tread carefully myself. If I talk in riddles, you can't blame me. I can't have anything come springing back at me." She paused. "And Phyllis?"

"Yes?"

"I have no idea where you're going to end up, but I pray nightly that Ronnie won't be in a cell either."

The tension lessened and Phyllis smiled. "I can live with that." She reached a hand over. "Would you prefer I never come back?"

Ann put down her cup, took Phyllis' hand. "If you never come back, how will I know how it ends?" Her small smile was there and gone.

"Somehow you seem to find things out from atop the little bookstore in Covent Gardens."

"Some news travels faster than others."

"By what means?"

The big grin spreading across Ann's face signaled the conversation was at a close. Okay, good enough.

When Phyllis gathered her few belongings, Ann went to a closet for a coat. Helping her into the sleeves, Ann rested a hand on Phyllis' arm.

"Before you go..."

"Yes?"

"I have one more thing for you and I'm done."

Phyllis waited by the door, clutching her purse and wrecked trench coat. She waited until Ann could look her in the face.

"Tell me, Ann. Ronnie's life depends on it."

"And that's the only reason I would tell you this but...there's a vault...in the basement of the Embassy and—"

"There's something important in it."

"I'd be surprised if certain files haven't been confiscated by the Army or whoever is investigating by now."

"Both Army and FBI are still investigating. They've taken offices on the second floor."

"Not surprising."

"What's in the vault, Ann?"

She hesitated before looking Phyllis in the eye. "Mr. Lawrence had me put certain files in there with the code name 'salamander' clearly on top."

"I was wondering when we'd get back to that."

"He would always tell me to not look at anything in the files, but to put them in there and get out as quickly as possible."

"Do you think those files were gathered by someone else? Could Ronnie have been slipping intelligence out that way?"

"I sure hope not, but whoever has the combination to the vault could be a suspect and potential problem."

Phyllis shook her head. "That's not going to help. Lots of people have the combination."

"Do you?"

That stopped her. "No. No, I don't, come to think of it." She stared back at Ann. "Why don't I as the secretary to the Military Attache?"

"Maybe Dick Simpson doesn't know what's in there either."

"So...you think I should check the files in the vault."

"I don't know that they're still there, but it's a possibility." She laid her hand on Phyllis' arm. "Whatever you do, be extra cautious and tell no one what you're doing. If the higher ups are keeping everyone away from the safe, it might be a forbidden place now— under military police protection."

She gave Phyllis a big hug. "Be careful and good luck."

Phyllis nodded. "Thanks. I will."
She took a deep breath and opened the door.

* * *

CHAPTER 22
The next day

"Why can't you meet me for dinner?"

"I told you, Joe. I brought some work home that needs to be done tonight."

"All right, then how about tomorrow night? We could go to Angel's. I hear Mick is bringing in a few musicians to play."

"You're kidding! Musicians?"

His silvery voice chuckled. "Well, one guy plays the harmonica and another has a violin. I can't imagine what kind of music they play together, but it should be interesting. And old John is serving Toad in the Hole."

"He must have gotten sausage from somewhere."

"John and Mick are certainly resourceful. How about it?"

Phyllis paused. It *did* sound like fun and she loved going to Angel's. After the rough week she'd had with Dickie anxiously ordering her around, plus her work for the Embassy's weekly memos, she could use a night out.

Wait a minute. There's that pesky vault to contend with. Damn.

"I'd really like to, Joe, but I just can't."

Silence on the line weighed her down. Why was she such a pushover for this guy? She was sorry to do it, but if he was seeing someone else…

"I don't understand." His quiet voice seemed almost sad. "Did I do something wrong, Phyllis?"

"Um…"

"Because I'd like the chance to straighten out whatever it is I did. Would you please let me?"

"Joe…"

"I thought we had a wonderful time at the Savoy." He lowered his voice. "When I kissed you, honey, I know you kissed me back. Don't you like me, Phyllis?"

Oh boy. The words stuck in her throat.

"I…I do, Joe. That's not the problem."

"Then please tell me what the problem is."

She rubbed her forehead, tugged on an ear. She scratched her scrunched nose and felt her body tingling all over from the lies she had to tell him. It didn't seem right.

"Can we have this conversation a little later? I have a headache and much work to do. Let me call you in a day or two when I know more."

"When you know more about what?"

Oops.

"Phyllis!" A loud voice called out. "Get off the phone! I need to use it!"

"Right away, Mrs. Stewart," Phyllis yelled back. Putting her ear to the receiver again, she could hear Joe's quiet breathing. She was so very tempted.

"I've got to go, Joe. Please give me some time."

He didn't speak right away. "Fine, but let me say this much: I like you very much, Phyllis, and I think you like me too. I'll give you some time, but not a lot. With this war, we don't know what tomorrow may bring and I'm not willing to waste an opportunity like this. I'll call you in two days."

"Um, Joe?" But she spoke to a dial tone as he'd already hung up. *Cheeky guy. Who did he think he was?*

Mrs. Stewart came up behind her and plucked the phone from her hand. "My turn. There was another car accident in blackout to call the authorities about."

"Won't the police already know?" Phyllis asked.

Mrs. Stewart snorted. "Not bloody likely. It happened while you were on the phone."

Phyllis turned to go back upstairs when the tiny landlady stopped her. "There's another letter from your cranky sister on the table. The mail is all but stopped but she still manages to chew you out every week or so."

"How would you know that?"

She smiled wickedly. "Steam, my dear. Steam."

Phyllis' mouth dropped open. "Ah, you can't just...why would you..." she stammered.

"There's a war on, dearie. Up to your room with you. That nosy Lorraine is waiting."

Shaking her head wearily, Phyllis went up the staircase, dragging one foot after the other. This day seemed to get worse with each passing minute. Her discussion with Lorraine couldn't wait, but she didn't want to have it either.

Might as well get it over with.

* * *

CHAPTER 23

"Sure took you long enough," Lorraine began. "I thought you were going to drop him. I heard you stammer and stall all the way up here."

Phyllis moved to the basin to splash cold water on her face. Reaching for a towel, she noted the reflection in the mirror was a curly-haired woman with dark circles under her eyes. The poor woman was worrying more and sleeping less. She patted her cheeks dry noting the blush of embarrassment that had crept up her smooth neck. Lying to Joe and putting him off seemed disloyal somehow, even with another woman in the picture. Deep inside, she felt she could trust him—other forces were at work here. She turned slowly to face her friend.

"What's with you tonight? You're not mad at him after all?"

"Lorraine." Phyllis plopped on the bed, kicked off her shoes. "Cut me a small break, would you?"

"Answer the question. We have a lot to discuss and I need to know how you feel about this guy before we proceed. I'm not sure about him."

Phyllis tucked a pillow under her head. "Okay, here it is—I don't know how I feel about him. He seems genuine when we're together and I think I can trust him. I hope I can trust him."

"What about the woman he met at the train station?"

She considered the question. "I'm willing, at this moment, to not take it on face value."

"Meaning?"

"I hope there's a reasonable explanation and he will give it to me, but I have bigger fish to fry right now."

"I'll say."

"Lorraine," her eyes softly pleaded, "I'm up to my neck playing Sherlock Holmes and it would be nice to have a sturdy man at my back."

"Gotcha. I could feel him out for you."

"No, I'll do it. You won't get anything out of him that he doesn't want out."

A mischievous sparkle lit Lorraine's eyes. "I've done fairly well with guys half his size."

"But not half his stature. Leave him to me."

"If you say so." She glanced down at Phyllis' hands. "You gonna read that letter now?"

"Yeah."

Ripping open the envelope, Phyllis read for a few minutes. Tears slid down the sides of her face and she sat up.

"What is it?"

She sniffled with more tears leaking from watery eyes. "My dad's in worse shape. Mary Ellen doesn't think he's going to last much longer." Looking at Lorraine, she wiped her nose. "I've got to go home."

"Now? In the middle of your case with Ronnie stuck in the brig, you have to leave?"

"Lorraine, he's my father. I have to." She threw her legs over the side of the bed and stood up to open a dresser. Phyllis began to toss underwear and other clothing over her shoulder.

"You can't leave right now!" Lorraine grabbed the clothing and threw it into the drawer as fast as Phyllis brought it out.

"Quit that!"

"Don't tell me what to do!"

"Well, you're not listening to anyone else so it's my job!"

They tugged on a flannel nightgown between them. "Give me that or else I'll…"

"Or else you'll what" Lorraine jerked it from Phyllis who had leaned away trying to gain an advantage. Without the tension, she fell backwards onto her butt.

"Ow! Look what you did! You ripped it."

Lorraine shoved the rest of the clothes back into the dresser and slammed it shut. She stood in front and crossed her arms across her chest. "Would you listen to me?"

"Briefly. Get on with it."

"You've got a lot of your plate, I realize. There's neurotic Dickie, loveable Joe, your sick father and jailbird Ronnie. Lie back down and let's discuss the next step calmly."

Phyllis glared at her, but dutifully lay on the soft bed. She closed her eyes when Lorraine began speaking.

"Can we put aside Dickie and Joe for the time being? With time pressing let's concentrate on Ronnie so you can go see your dad."

She thought that over. "Maybe. What else?"

"I think we may find some answers in the vault, like Ann suggested. If we work together, I can get you in there."

Phyllis' eyes blinked open, slid to watch Lorraine. "How? Even Dickie doesn't have the combination."

"Which is strange, is it not?" Lorraine cocked her head. "The Military Attache of the American Embassy doesn't know the combination to a vault where important papers are placed."

"…Maybe he's been so busy that he…"

"And how do you know for sure he doesn't have it?"

"I asked him today on the pretense of needing something for the FBI."

"So you lied to your boss."

Phyllis shrugged. "Desperate times call for desperate measures. I've heard that Ronnie may be sent back to the States soon for proceedings to begin. If I don't do something now, the opportunities are going to dry up hard and fast."

"I agree." She sat on the bed, looked across the room. "Man, it's chilly in here. Did you forget to light the fireplace again?"

120

"Ah…"

"Oh, never mind. I'll do it while we talk." Lorraine rose to put loose paper on the fireplace logs. She reached up for the matches and glanced back at Phyllis.

"I know where I can get my hands on the combination."

Phyllis pushed up on her elbows. "Where?"

"Let me worry about that for now." Once the fire was going, Lorraine walked back to sit on a chair by the desk. "What we need to talk about first is how you can manage being locked in a vault without freaking out."

"And secondly?"

"What to look for when you're in there."

"I'll do fine in the vault but why will you need to lock me in?"

"In case someone walks by. I can't just stand guard by an open door. That door is locked around the clock; you go in to do your business and you go out quickly with someone always there."

"So what's the procedure?"

"I'll get you in, shut the door and keep a lookout for anyone coming close." She smirked. "I may have to use my wily ways to keep some guy away."

Phyllis smiled. "I'm sure that won't be a hardship for you."

Lorraine returned her smile. "Anyway, I figure five minutes in is all we can risk."

"Five minutes. Inside a locked vault."

"Yes, can you handle it?"

A shudder worked its way slowly down her body. Phyllis sat up with beads of sweat popping out on her forehead.

"I know it won't be easy, but this is necessary, right?"

Phyllis swallowed hard. "Right. Just don't forget about me or it could be curtains. Lights out, certainly."

Lorraine rose, headed for the door. "Get some sleep. We'll do this tomorrow night."

"That soon?"

"You bet."

"I feel like I'm being pushed through a meat grinder."

"Then suck it in, friend. You're going to need all your wits about you."

She nodded. "Close the door on your way out."

"Aren't you going to change?"

Phyllis sank into the comforter tucking it tightly around her. "Nope. You ripped my nightie in our game of tug 'o war, remember?"

Lorraine flicked the light switch dimming the warm room. "Night, sweetie."

* * *

CHAPTER 24

So many things could go wrong, but Lorraine was going to make sure they didn't.

She knew Phyllis was probably scared stiff to be in a closed, darkened vault for any length of time and briefly considered trading places with her. Problem was...Phyllis knew what to look for. Lorraine knew her friend was holding out certain pieces of information, but that was all right. This was her show and she would support Phyllis as much as humanly possible.

Now...returning to the plot at hand.

Lorraine worked on the first floor in an office off a side hallway. She had a clear view of anyone going the next level down where the vault was located. Since her job had become occasional liaison with the FBI, she sometimes accompanied them downstairs to let them in certain offices and to run messages between the FBI and her boss, one of the Embassy accountants. And she'd become friendly enough with the FBI, that her presence was welcomed. For such standoffish men, they accepted her almost as part of the furniture, only prettier. She'd seen the looks of appreciation and was hoping to use them to her benefit.

The next day Lorraine was hard at work at her desk when Byron, the cutest of the FBI bunch, asked her to accompany him downstairs. He didn't seem to really need anything, but was on his lunch hour and bored. She smiled knowing she could be good company for a while. Just long enough. Going in to tell her boss she'd be gone, Lorraine asked him softly to call her on the downstairs phone after five minutes.

"Why?" her boss asked. Kevin wasn't the brightest of bulbs, but a nice enough sort.

She tilted her head toward the door. "I'm going down with Byron. I want an excuse to come back."

"Oh. Oh, sure. I get it." He winked at her conspiratorially.

Lorraine and Byron chatted amiably walking down the stairs to the basement level.

"So that's where you're from. I've heard Florida is beautiful."

"Have you ever been there?" He laughed. "It's hot, muggy and full of bugs in the summer. Winter's nice though."

"Sounds like an interesting place."

Rounding a corner, they came to a large open room. "You've been down here before, right, Lorraine?"

She smiled sweetly. "Many times. I was in the vault room with your partner, Sam, the other day."

"Is that why he had a big old smile on his face the rest of the day," Bryon teased. He had the classic movie star face, probably too handsome for his own good.

"And why are all you FBI men so good-looking? Is that a requirement for the service?"

"Yes, ma'am," he laughed. "Just like Embassy women are required to be gorgeous."

She ducked her head, blushing. "Oh, you shouldn't tease me like that, you meanie."

They walked into a small room with dimmed lighting and furniture pushed out of the way. It didn't look utilized.

"You getting something out of the vault, Byron?"

"Yes. I hope you don't mind keeping me company. Today's been rather slow."

"Oh, I can imagine. You work so hard." She rubbed his arm slowly. Up and down. The look he gave her nearly melted her resolve.

"Stand back here, Lorraine, honey. I need to unlock it."

"Okay."

She stood a few feet behind as Bryon reached into a pocket for a slip of paper. Reading it, he stuffed it back in and reached for the combination lock. Bryon's long fingers twirled the knob left stopping at a number, then right stopping again and lastly left for a third number. The mechanism clicked and the heavy vault door swung open.

"Open says me," joked Bryon.

She watched him go in, moving some papers around before plucking a box from a shelf. He walked back out shutting the door firmly behind him. She spied a water cooler close by and walked over to fill a paper cup. Taking a sip, she licked her lips seductively as Bryon watched her closely.

"Let me have some."

"Sure." She took a step towards him with her arm extended to give him the cup. A wall phone began to ring shrilly startling them both. Lorraine stumbled, tossing the water all over Byron's suit jacket. His mouth formed a big O as he looked incredulously from his drenched jacket back to a sheepish Lorraine.

She picked up the phone.

"Yes? Oh, sure. It's for you." She handed him the receiver.

"Hello?"

"Let me help you out of that wet jacket, Byron." Lorraine murmured sweetly slipping his arms out of the sleeves. He twisted around with the phone stuck to his ear and she took the jacket off him.

"Um, okay, if you want. That's it?" When he turned away from her, Lorraine quickly took the paper out of his inside pocket, memorized the numbers. She slipped it back in as he hung up the phone.

"That was the darndest thing."

"What was?" She continued to brush water from his jacket.

"Your boss wanted me to tell you he needs you upstairs."

"Oh," she laughed. "That's Kevin. He's kind of goofy sometimes, always playing practical jokes. It might be on you this time."

Bryon's brows furrowed but the picture must have seemed all right because he soon smiled. "Let me take that. You shouldn't be caught holding my jacket...wouldn't look right."

She arched a brow. "It would look just fine, Bryon."

He laughed out loud, took her arm to escort her upstairs. "You busy tonight, Lorraine?"

"You're a pretty cheeky fellow."

"Well, are you?"

"Yes, I am, but tomorrow I'm free."

"What a break because I am too."

She moved closer. "So where are you taking me?"

"Blue Anchor?"

"You read my mind."

* * *

CHAPTER 25

"You're strangely calm for what we're about to do."

"Do I have a choice?"

"Proud of you, sweetie and I'll have the whiskey on tap when we're out of here."

Phyllis shook her head. "Just get me home."

The American Embassy looked as dark inside as outside when Lorraine and Phyllis made their way to the back of the building. Mitch, an MP, was on duty tonight but was fortunately sound asleep in a chair positioned by the door. Phyllis quietly inserted her key, but a tiny click from the opening door made them freeze. Mitch's eyes remained firmly closed, although he shifted somewhat in his chair causing Phyllis' heart to stop.

Protection seemed light tonight possibly because Lt. Col. Lawrence was heading stateside soon. With the case apparently hardening against him, Lorraine and Phyllis knew it was only a matter of days before whatever they did made no difference.

Once inside, shadows loomed in abstract shapes on the floor and walls. As they walked through the silent building, soft squeaks from their sneakers echoed alarmingly down the hallway. Phyllis hurried along.

"Wait up," said Lorraine.

"Shh. Keep a lid on the talking."

"Okay."

They hurried down the staircase leading to the basement that Lorraine had visited earlier in the day with Byron. It was darker in the lower level, if that were possible, causing anxiety levels to rise. Lorraine reached for Phyllis' hand.

"Your hands are ice, Phyl," she whispered.

"No kidding. Yours aren't toasty either."

"That would be because I'm scared down to my sneakers."

"Me too." Phyllis stopped suddenly. "It's not too late to go home. No harm done."

Lorraine tugged her hand forward into the vault room. "No can do. We're here now. Let's do what we came to do."

Just then footsteps were heard running up the stairs! Couldn't be Mitch! They'd left him outside fast asleep. Phyllis pushed Lorraine against the wall and flattened herself as well. In the dark, she knew they hadn't been seen, but wondered who else was roaming the halls of the Embassy long past the hour when most people were in bed. It was after midnight and they had no business being here. The military police would have flipped on a light, so someone else had no business being here either.

They held their breath to listen as the footsteps grew softer, until there was no sound at all. Only then did Phyllis suck in a gulp of air.

"You okay?"

"No," Lorraine spoke to the wall. "My heart stopped full stop."

"Who the hell was that?"

"Whoever it was didn't want to be identified."

"That sure makes me wonder why."

"We could run after them."

Phyllis shook her head. "Not a good idea. We might run into Mitch. Besides, what if they have a gun?"

"Yeah, well, there's that."

Lorraine pushed away from the wall squinting in the dark.

"Did you bring a flashlight?"

"I did."

"...So let's get to work."

Lorraine stopped in front of the vault. Reaching back for Phyllis' hand, she squeezed tight and whispered, "You sure you want to go through with this?"

"I'm sure, but this wasn't what I had in mind when I put in for the transfer to London. How about you?"

"We're fighting a different kind of war...covert."

Phyllis nudged her. "Do it."

Lorraine handed Phyllis the light. "Hold this for me."

With a steady beam directed at the combination lock, Lorraine slowly twisted the knob left, right, then left. She was precise with each number and tried to keep her hand steady with each rotation. Wiping sweat from her brow, the last number caused the mechanism to click loudly before a bolt slid back and the heavy metal door began to swing open. Lorraine pulled it open completely and they peered inside. With no lights, the darkness was absolute.

"Good thing you brought that flashlight."

"Yeah," Phyllis cleared her throat. "Show time."

In the doorway, she hesitated. Over a shoulder, she nodded to Lorraine. "Don't forget about me, okay?"

"Five minutes."

"Five minutes."

* * *

CHAPTER 26

This was easily the longest five minutes of her life. When the door closed behind her, Phyllis had to concentrate on breathing short puffs of air in an effort to keep from feeling woozy. She could feel her anxiety level kicking up a notch, but was determined to see the job through.

Searching in the dark with a tiny light, she could see the space was not particularly large but there was room for a small table tucked into the corner by the door. Phyllis caught her foot on a table leg and nearly tumbled to the floor. Righting herself, she cupped her hands around her mouth trying to keep from hyperventilating. Further searching showed a pile of bags in another corner by a small wastebasket.

It was stuffy with air so stale she didn't want to breathe it in. The only things in the vault were three rows of shelves and a filing cabinet pushed to one side. Holding her breath, Phyllis searched the various folders stacked on the shelves before turning her attention to the filing cabinet. She pulled on the handle finding it locked. No matter. Feeling around on the shelf above it, Phyllis easily found the small key thoughtfully hidden by some secretary who had probably forgotten hers once and left it so she wouldn't have to trek back upstairs for another. She shined her light inside each drawer of the cabinet finding little of interest. Past information about the war effort might be interesting, but nothing worth being charged with espionage. Only current information would be worth the risk.

Or maybe the FBI had removed the sensitive material before she even got here. Disappointed, she perched on the table, trying to keep from beating on the vault door for Lorraine to let her out. With her pulse pounding and her breathing limited, she wondered what to do next. It all seemed like a big, fat waste of time until she allowed herself a bigger breath and…her nose picked up another smell.

Acidic.

The smell of ammonia. Strange. Why would the inside of a vault smell like ammonia?

Shining her tiny pinprick of light in every part of the small space, her light reflected off the bags by the wastebasket. Through her haze, it occurred to her that there were too many bags or maybe it was just one big one. She hopped off the table, walking five steps to see what was there. On closer examination, it appeared to be a large shiny overcoat, possibly gabardine. Her foot stepped into some liquid spilled on the floor. When she shined the light down, the bottom of her shoe was covered with blood! The acidic smell mixed with a sweetly metallic scent and suddenly Phyllis was woozy, on sensory overload.

It was hard enough to be enclosed in a stuffy space, but finding blood and…oh, my God! *Was that a body?* Her light wobbled when it reflected along the lumpy overcoat coming to rest on a puffy, familiar face. She stumbled back trying desperately to get away from him, the smells, the walls closing in until her periphery vision narrowed and she passed out cold.

"Phyllis! Phyllis! Wake up!"

A chilly hand was patting her face, now thoroughly moistened and dripping. More liquid trickled on her cheeks and eyes causing her to blink rapidly as she stirred.

"What happened?"

"You fainted, sweetie."

"Am I still in the vault?"

"No, I opened it to find you stretched out by the dead guy. I dragged you out."

"Oh, man…what a nightmare!"

Lorraine helped her sit up. "Here. Drink this."

"What is it?"

"Water. It'll help bring you around."

Phyllis stretched her legs out on the floor as she drank down the cool water. It did help. Soon she was feeling close to normal until her mind came back to the contents of the vault. She pushed herself up, but wobbled on her feet. Lorraine grabbed her arm.

"Whoa! Not so fast, slugger. You hit your head when you went down."

She reached up a hand to feel a sore spot. "No wonder my head's killing me."

"Hey! Where are you going?"

"Back into the vault."

Lorraine's eyes bugged out. "Why? Let's get out of here!"

"No, wait."

"Wait for what?"

But Phyllis had already hurried back into the vault, this time leaving the door wide open. The air was still stale with a sickeningly sweet scent but she had to do this.

"Hold that light, Lorraine. I'm going to check him."

"No! Don't touch him."

"I'll be careful but I have to see who it is."

She pulled Ann's hanky from her pocket to wrap around her hand. Hovering above the body, Phyllis moved the face. "It *is* him."

"Who?" Lorraine asked from behind her.

"Silas Reardon."

"You can fill me in on who the heck that is later."

She searched his pockets with her covered hand and found another slip of paper with numbers on it. She put it in her pocket. Checking a billfold in his jacket, she found Dickie's business card and an IOU on a napkin with Blue Anchor stamped in the middle. *Blue Anchor?* There was also three hundred dollars in cash as well as three hundred British pounds.

Putting everything else back where she found it, Phyllis was ready to go until Lorraine's unsteady light shined on something else.

"Lorraine. Steady."

132

"Okay. Where?"

"On his hand."

She pried loose a finger from the clenched fist. Shiny strands of hair were caught between his fingers.

"Lorraine, look. What color is that hair?"

"I'm not sure. Kind of blondish?"

"Nope. You're not looking closely enough. Try again."

Lorraine crouched down to get a closer look. Squinting, she cocked her head to one side. "Red, maybe?"

Phyllis nodded, rose to her feet. "No maybe."

* * *

CHAPTER 27
The next morning

"You want to know the last thing on my mind before I passed out in the vault?"

"Tell me."

"I was with my grandmother."

"Oh, Phyllis, no…"

"I was five and…"

"You don't need to say it out loud."

"I do need to say it out loud, Lorraine, because it won't leave my brain until I do."

"Go."

Someone began pounding on Phyllis' door. "Hey! You awake, Phyl? You're going to be late for work."

"Thanks, Doris," she called out. "I'm almost ready."

Phyllis looked in her mirror, brushed a little burnt cork on her eyelashes and picked up her powder. Smoothing her cheeks, she looked over at Lorraine who nodded.

"You were five."

"Right." She blew out a breath. "I was sitting by my grandmother's coffin in the funeral parlor because I was waiting for her to get up so we could go. Someone," she stopped, licked her lips, "turned off the lights. My family was large with five children and my parents apparently forgot me."

"Huh."

"So I sat by the coffin in the dark for I don't know how long, it could have been only a few minutes, but it seemed like a lifetime. I was so scared I didn't know what to do...should I run? Should I hide?"

"What did you do?" Lorraine handed a brush to her.

"I hid under my grandmother's coffin until the lights flicked on and my mother pulled me out." Her eyes slid to her friend. "I've had a fear of tight places ever since."

"Maybe you should get therapy."

"Maybe so."

They walked to work together that day, dodging the mannequin pieces in front of the clothing store. They talked about the fine day, for once it wasn't raining, and talked about the work waiting for them, but they couldn't seem to talk about what happened last night until they were nearly to the Embassy.

"What about him?"

Phyllis knew who she meant. "I'm not sure. Got any ideas? It should be reported, but how? We're not supposed to know he's in there."

"Plus we don't want to alert the killer."

They looked at each other wide-eyed. "Hope he didn't see us."

"Or her. I'll get Kevin to look in there for some reason or another."

"Won't that scare him? Poor Kev is not the bravest of men."

"True but I'll be there to hold his hand. He'll be all right."

"Okay then."

Lorraine opened the heavy front door to the American Embassy. The stiff-lipped MP at the door waved them in.

"What happens now?"

Phyllis walked in, took off her jacket. "Let me think about it."

"Better you than me."

* * *

135

CHAPTER 28

"Phyllis? I need you!" Dickie's voice resonated down the hallway. He sounded upset.

"Yes, sir. I was right in the outer office."

"Yeah, well," he sputtered. "Didn't hear you come in."

She stood in front of his messy desk, steno pad in hand. "Do you need me for dictation?"

"I...ah, that is..." He went through piles of paper on his desk before opening a few drawers and checking them as well. Next he rose, looked under his chair before settling back down, still antsy.

"Need me to come back?"

"No, no. Take this letter."

She perched on the chair and readied her pad. Licking the point of her pencil, she was poised to write.

"To Major Garrett, Supplies, Washington, D.C. Dear Wallace," he began. When he stopped, she looked up at him.

"Sir?"

"Can you read that back, please?"

"Um, okay. Major Garrett, Supplies, Washington, D.C. Dear Wallace."

"That's not the whole address."

"But that's all you told me, sir."

He seemed lost. She studied him as he studied his hands. Something was off about Dickie today. His tie was askew and he had dark sweat stains under his arms. He looked nervous and she had a funny feeling she knew why.

"Are you all right, Major Simpson?"

"I, ah...no, Phyllis. Actually, I'm not."

"Anything I can do to help you?"

"Is there any water left in the pitcher?"

"I'll check." She got up to check the water in a pitcher sitting on a nearby table. After pouring him a cup, Phyllis handed it to him. He drank it down in one long swallow and handed the cup back to her.

When he'd gathered himself, he opened his mouth. "Did you hear?"

"Hear what, sir?"

"About the murder?"

She hoped her face was set to neutral. "No. What happened?"

"Kevin from downstairs found a body in the vault this morning."

"Really?" She wasn't a good actress and hoped she gave nothing away. "Has the body been identified?"

"It's someone you may have seen around here occasionally. His name is, was Silas Reardon."

"I remember him in here talking to you one time but I don't know him."

"You saw him in here?"

"Once, a while back. Why?"

"Phyllis, if you're questioned about him, you don't have to mention that."

She blinked at him. "Are you asking me to lie?" *What was this about?*

"No, no, of course not, but if no one asks," he added cautiously, "just don't volunteer the information."

She stared at him long and hard. "Major Simpson. That request smacks of guilt. You guilty about something?"

"No, ma'am," he said quickly wiping moisture from his upper lip. "He wasn't someone I wanted around is all."

"Why is that?"

"Phyllis, if I say something to you, can you keep it to yourself?"

"Certainly, sir. I deal with classified materials all the time."

"Yes, yes," he waved his hand, "but this is different."

"How so?"

"First Lt. Col. Lawrence is arrested for espionage and now a murder on premise. So saying there's a problem at the Embassy is a massive understatement and Reardon may have been part of it."

"Do you think Mr. Lawrence did what he's been accused of?"

"Absolutely not! Ronnie was the most loyal and patriotic officer I've had the pleasure to work with. He'd never do anything as sinister as this."

"As sinister as what?"

She slid her eyes to a small brush on the desk. Pale hair clung to the bristles giving her pause. Was it red?

"Phyllis? You look like you've seen a ghost."

"No, sir," she swallowed. "But I have a theory about Mr. Lawrence, if you'd care to hear it."

He leaned back in his chair, waved at her to sit. "By all means."

"Since no one I know thinks he's guilty of spying, I think he was being blackmailed."

Dickie paled, rose to get another cup of water. He chugged it and glanced shyly back at her. "What...what gives you that idea?"

Hoping this didn't come flinging back at her, Phyllis took a breath and continued. "It doesn't add up. The man is a high-ranking officer in the U.S. Army and has the distinguished position of Military Attache at the American Embassy in London, right smack dab in the middle of the war with Germany."

"So he's in a good place should he decide to be a spy," he prompted.

"Yes, but unless he's a very good actor, I can't see him pulling it off. He has a family here that would suffer dire consequences if he were caught. They are suffering those consequences with Mrs. Lawrence screaming his innocence to anyone who will listen."

"That doesn't mean he didn't do it."

"So you have certain doubts then, Major Simpson?"

"No, of course not."

"Because I get the feeling that something is going on, sir, right under our very noses. Why else would there a dead man in the vault? And why else would his name cause you distress?"

Dickie straightened in his chair, trying to maintain a neutral expression. He picked up a few papers, shuffled them in a pile and placed them neatly aside.

"That'll be all, Miss Bowden. We'll finish the letter later."

"Yes, sir." She rose from the chair, turned to leave.

"And Phyllis?"

"Sir?"

"Let's forget about this conversation, shall we?"

She shrugged. "Yes, sir."

Not bloody likely.

* * *

CHAPTER 29

"I swear I see redheads everywhere we go."

Phyllis laughed but her eyes scanned continuously. She and Lorraine were walking down two blocks to the State Department building. They were going back to see Willie Winter with the new information they had. Phyllis knew he'd go haywire when he saw her, so she brought Lorraine to keep him under control, or at least happy. She did have a way with men, Phyllis had to admit.

"Norma's a redhead."

They nodded at a bobby walking past. "You've got to be kidding. You think Norma, petite Norma, who must be a whole one hundred and ten pounds soaking wet could overpower and stab Reardon? He was a beefy guy."

Phyllis turned to stare. "That's what happened?"

"Yes. Mitch, the MP at the door told me."

"Martha in the steno pool has red hair."

Lorraine chuckled, stepping off the curb to cross the street. "You'd like it to be Martha since she was so snobby to you that day in the Officers' Mess."

"Not at all. She's been fine lately, although the murder has everyone on pins and needles."

"That's putting it mildly."

Phyllis quickened her pace to stay in step. The street was lined with the rubble of bombed out cafes and stores. People picked their way cautiously looking for anything of value. Children were subdued playing in the shadows of once important buildings. Even with a clear sky, no one seemed to be in a good mood and the importance of the moment wasn't lost to her.

"Life's changed so much for the British people." She glanced around her at the destruction. "I don't remember the death total for this week, do you?"

Lorraine shivered, clutched her coat around her tightly. "No. Nothing will be the same for any of us."

They walked briskly down another block before speaking.

"The Queen of England has red hair."

Phyllis glanced at Lorraine and they burst out laughing.

"No way did the Queen stab that guy. She's a little busy keeping up the people's morale."

"True. Pickings are slim," chuckled Lorraine.

"Doesn't that other MP have red hair? What's his name? Pete?"

"Peter Cummings."

"Of course, you'd know his name."

Lorraine pouted. "You know lots of the boys in this country too."

"Not as many as you do, my friend. Anyway," she continued, "you think Pete did it?"

"What reason would he have?"

"Maybe he's the spy." Lorraine opened her mouth to interrupt. "No, wait. I might be on to something here. He frames Ronnie and cuts a deal with Silas about selling secrets to the highest bidder. He's got motive and he's on site."

"There's so many holes in that theory, I can't even tell you."

"For instance?"

"How do you know Reardon was involved? That information in his hand could have been planted. Pete's a loyal soldier; he'd never commit an act of treason."

"You so sure?"

"Yes. Let's discount both Silas and Pete."

"Forget Pete," said Phyllis. "But it seems logical that Reardon was involved in some way because he was found someplace he shouldn't have been, was murdered and we found that note in his pocket."

Lorraine stopped, put her hand on Phyllis' arm. "We shouldn't have removed that, you know. It was evidence and might have led to whoever killed him."

Phyllis nudged her along. "We'll deal with that later, but I agree about Pete. Let's think of another redhead."

"Malcolm has red hair."

"Malcolm?"

"At the Blue Anchor."

"Unlikely. Isn't he in Scotland right now?"

"He left a few days ago to visit his mother."

"What a nice man." Phyllis smiled.

"The mayor of London has red hair." Phyllis rolled her eyes.

They turned a corner; the State Department was in sight.

"If you glance around, Phyllis, a quarter of the population in London has red hair and probably half of England, not to mention Ireland and Scotland. That was a crummy clue for Silas to leave us."

Phyllis chuckled, got out her identification for the guard at the gate. "Next time I talk to him, I'll pass along your complaint."

After the guard waved them in, the women entered the building and headed down the first flight of stairs they came to.

"Is this a shortcut? It's not the way I came the last time."

Lorraine pointed to a camera in the middle of the room. "We'll get caught on camera if we go that way and Willie will beat it out of here faster than you can say *jack rabbit.*"

"Ha. Okay." But it almost happened.

* * *

CHAPTER 30

"Oh, no you don't! Grab him, Phyl, before he gets out the door!"

Willie emitted a shriek when Phyllis tackled him and they fell in a heap on the slick floor in the dim basement of the State Department.

"Where do you think you're going, Wee Willie?"

"That's Wise Willie to you, Lorraine."

"With Phyllis parked on your back, you don't seem so wise."

"Let me up." His muffled voice sounded scratchy and irritated.

"Not unless you promise to help us."

"No dice," he shot back. "You two are up to no good and you're going to get me in trouble too."

"How about," Lorraine's voice softened and her southern accent floated in the air, "you give us five minutes and we'll be out of your hair forever."

He turned his reddened face toward her with a scowl. "How about you get out of my hair now and I won't call the guard."

But Lorraine continued soothingly. "How about I take you out to the Blue Anchor for a nightcap tomorrow? I know your favorite brand of ale generally stocked there." She pouted with seductive red lips. "Mmm? Pretty please? You know we'll have a few laughs, Willie. Don't we usually?"

His face softened with a smile blooming eventually. "Well…"

Phyllis rolled her eyes and slid off Willie's back. Lorraine shook her head with a finger to her lips.

"Five minutes, Wise Willie?"

He pushed up, smiled at Lorraine but glared at Phyllis. "Does she have to be with us?" He jerked his thumb in Phyllis' direction.

"She'll be quiet as a mouse."

"All right, then. Let's head back to my office."

Walking down the dark hallway, Lorraine asked, "How'd you see us? We came the side way."

"Cameras there too, ladies."

"Well, thanks for meeting us anyway," said Phyllis.

"Yeah," he scoffed, "like I had a choice with you two."

He unlocked the door to his office and walked inside, waited for Lorraine and Phyllis to follow, then locked the door behind them.

"Locking us in?" asked Lorraine.

"Taking no chances," he mumbled heading for his desk. "Have a seat."

As soon as Phyllis was seated, she reached into her purse and pulled out a slip of paper. He regarded it warily as she handed it to him.

"I shudder to ask, but is this another encrypted message?"

"I think so."

Willie's shoulders shook for a tense moment. Wiping a hand down his jeans, he reached hesitantly for the paper being thrust in his direction. "I feel like one of our soldiers stepping lightly between land mines."

Lorraine cocked her head. "Learning empathy is never a bad thing."

The message looked similar to the other note. Willie's eyes darted to Phyllis. "What did you do with the other one? Burn it, like I suggested?"

"Actually," Phyllis responded sheepishly, "I forgot about it and still have it here in my purse."

Both Lorraine and Willie looked shocked with wide, frightened eyes. He literally backed his chair away from her and his hands shot out defensively in front of him.

"I can't help either of you!" He stood quickly, knocking his chair over behind him.

Lorraine walked over to right his chair. She tugged him back onto the seat while patting his shoulder soothingly. "Now Willie. It'll be fine. How about we burn both notes right here after you've translated the second one?"

He made a motion to hop up again, but she kept him sitting. "You can't do that in my office! Why, someone will smell it and wonder what's up."

"Not at all, Willie honey." Lorraine glanced at Phyllis. "Do you have that little bit of perfume left from the bottle that Cliff at the base gave you?"

Phyllis fished around in her purse to bring out a small, delicate bottle. She held it high. "Here it is!"

Willie looked flabbergasted with slacked jaw and disbelieving eyes. "You two are nuts!"

"Willie," Lorraine picked up his pencil to hand to him. "Wise Willie," she cooed. "Please translate this note and we'll get out of here so fast you won't remember we were here." She ruffled his disheveled mop of hair as he shook his head.

"I'll do it to get rid of you both."

Taking the pencil from Lorraine, she stepped back as he reached into a bottom drawer for his cipher book. Skimming through several pages, he came to a stop and ran a finger down the page. Scanning the information, he poised his pencil with the haunted eyes of a man on the verge of a nervous breakdown. Willie began to scratch words on a pad of paper glancing alternately at the note and book. After several minutes of intense writing, he wearily passed his translation over to Phyllis.

"You know what you have to do with that, don't you?" he asked cautiously.

"What?"

"Turn it over to the Military Attache. He's in charge and the first in your chain of command."

Without responding, Phyllis looked at the slip of paper in her hand. Lorraine walked over to read over her shoulder. They read through what he'd written and looked over at him.

"What does this mean, Willie?"

"If I had to guess…"

"Please do," added Lorraine.

"I'd say that someone has been compiling lists of weaponry that will be left when the war is over." He nodded to Phyllis. "See the lists?"

"Yes."

"This war began with Allied soldiers using bolt action rifles. In fact, it's that kind of weapon that has been a mainstay for many nations involved."

"So?"

"As the war has progressed, new production methods for weapons have been developed, so now we have semi-automatic rifles, assault rifles, and sub-machine guns being manufactured by Germans, Japanese, British and American companies." He stopped. "Do you follow?"

"What's so secret about that?"

He nodded towards her paper. "What you have in your hand is a list of weaponry, where it can be located and how much is being charged for it."

"So that means…" began Lorraine.

"Someone has already started war-profiteering before the war has even ended. They need to be stopped, Lorraine, because it's treason against the Allied forces. If supply officers are selling the equipment instead of sending it out to use in battles, it's unlawful and immoral."

Lorraine looked sick. "I can't even imagine why somebody would do such a horrible thing."

"For money, Lorraine," said Phyllis. "That's the bottom line although if Silas Reardon was one of the carriers of information, I suspect he was in it for another reason as well."

"What reason?"

Phyllis shook her head. "We'll get into that later. I want to get a bit more information before I float that theory."

She wadded the paper and stuck it in her purse by the other note.

"Will you burn those now?" pleaded Willie.

"No." She held up a hand to stop Willie's protest. "If this is happening in the American Embassy under our noses, I'm going to need these as evidence."

"You can get into so much trouble if that information is found on you." Willie glanced at Lorraine who nearly withered.

"Phyllis? You sure you know what you're doing?"

"I hope so." She rose, stuck out a hand. "Thank you, Willie. Wise Willie." She smiled. "You won't see us again and we were never here."

"Gotcha." A slow smile spread across his face. "Although I could be coerced to be a character witness at your trial."

* * *

CHAPTER 31

"So where you going to stow the dynamite now residing in between those slaps of leather?"

"Someplace safe."

"There is no place safe. What if a bad guy knows you're on to them?"

"I'll leave a note with Mrs. Stewart where this information can be found."

"Then," added Lorraine with a shake of her head, "you're putting Mrs. Stewart at risk."

"She won't know what the information is. I'll just leave her an envelope with a note telling her where to find it all, if something happens to me."

Lorraine shivered and not just from the sudden wind that had picked up on their way home. "Scary thought. Waking up this morning, it occurred to me that I was Dr. Watson to your Sherlock Holmes."

Phyllis smiled, tucked her arm in Lorraine's. "And as such you need to do as I say."

"Watson wrote down Holmes' exploits in the newspaper."

"Which you can do, if you want, after this is all over."

"But I probably won't be able to since all this stuff is hush-hush," she countered.

It was nearly blackout time and they nodded to a bobby passing by. Stepping onto their long block of red brick row houses, Phyllis noticed the covered streetlamps and dark curtains in the windows. Trees were beginning to bud with bits of grass poking through in some small plots around the sidewalks. Their block had been spared much of the buzz bomb damage and for that she was grateful. Her little corner of London seemed almost normal with the fog settling over the town like a fine mist. She and Lorraine chattered away until she noticed the man standing on the doorstep of Seven Addison Bridge Place.

Joe.

Phyllis chugged to a halt stopping Lorraine with her.

"What?"

"Look."

Lorraine swerved her head in the direction Phyllis pointed. She giggled softly. "Well, you knew he was going to show up sooner or later, didn't you?" She walked on ahead. "I'll invite him in."

"Lorraine..." she began but her friend paid no attention. Phyllis watched her wave at Joe and open the front door to let him in. He remained where he was, however, waiting for her. She involuntarily smiled that he would want to wait for her. Inside her shoes, her toes curled at the delicious thought.

"It's been two days." Joe returned her smile with a cocky one of his own.

"So it has." *A productive two days actually.*

Even with the open door and Mrs. Stewart sneaking a peek, Joe tugged her to him and planted a noisy smooch on her willing lips.

"Glad to see me?"

"You know everyone in the house is probably watching."

He smiled against her lips. "Let 'em watch. They're all jealous."

"Maybe so."

Joe kissed her again before releasing her. "Invite me in?"

"I believe Lorraine already did that, but sure, Joe. Come on in." She started to walk inside, but stopped abruptly. Joe nearly bumped into her.

"What's up, Phyllis?"

"On second thought," she turned, dragged him outside shutting the door. "Let's have a pint down at the pub on the corner, I need to talk to you about something."

149

He stood still watching her. A breeze ruffled his wavy hair and his dark eyes were curious. His height and stature might have been imposing to some, but to Phyllis, Joe Schneider was becoming more comfortable than her new set of Rosie-the-Riveter coveralls. That recognition swept through her like a cyclone causing her to shiver.

"Cold?" Joe began to take off his overcoat.

She shook her head. "No, I'm fine." Phyllis took his hand and started down the sidewalk with him.

"Where are we going?"

"Just to the corner. A little place called Meux's known for its old English beef."

Joe chuckled. "I sure hope Meux doesn't have it held over since old English times. That could be bad for digestion."

They made small talk on their way to the pub. He mentioned the changes at the State Department and Henry's promotion, while she tried to dodge his questions about the goings-on at the American Embassy. Reaching Meux's, Joe opened the door and peered in briefly before stepping aside for Phyllis.

"Looks harmless enough. Let's find a seat."

Phyllis walked in, spied a small table by the window. Joe shook his head.

"Nah. How about the one towards the back?"

"Sure."

After settling in, Joe went up to the bar for two pints of ale. She took stock of the few patrons sitting casually at the bar taking pulls of their beer. When Joe brought two frothy glasses of ale to their table, she reached for hers delightedly.

"I'm sure going to miss this when I go home."

"When will that be, do you think?" Joe blew off some of the foam before taking a good swallow.

"After the war, for sure. My father's ill and I need to see him."

"That's right. I hope it's nothing serious."

"Actually, it is, but that's not why I asked you to come with me tonight, Joe."

"I didn't think so, but it's nice to see you." His warm eyes roamed her face. "I've missed you."

Phyllis moved her chair closer to him. "Did you really? You're not shining me on, are you?"

His brows narrowed. "Why would I shine you on, honey? I'm happy just to be with you."

"And I'm happy to be with you, but it's a little scary."

"What is?"

"This is wartime. I'm fully aware that romances are quickly distinguished in the fog of war. Here today and gone tomorrow."

"Actually, I'm a little more interested in you than just a wartime romance, but if that's all you want, well..."

"Well, what?"

"I hope I can change your mind, I guess."

She sipped her ale and thought about that. Joe watched her carefully almost as if he were studying her expression. He definitely saw too much which unnerved her.

"I'm going out on a limb here."

"Okay."

"I hope I can trust you."

"You can."

She slumped in her chair and stared at a noisy customer up at the bar. He'd clinked his glass with another guy spilling beer all over his clothes. Instead of being upset, the two men laughed uproariously. She smiled despite herself.

"Phyllis? What's this about?"

"I...I...need your help, Joe. Can I count on you?"

He leaned in closer and softened his voice. "Are you in some kind of trouble?"

"I sure hope not, but the Embassy is in turmoil right now and I...I know a few things that maybe I shouldn't."

Silence wove a spell around them in the small pub. She never expected his response.

* * *

CHAPTER 32

"What kind of things? You can count on me."

He didn't run for the hills. It was exactly the right thing to say and she relaxed a bit, but still wondered how much to tell him. As darkness settled outside, the proprietor set up candles on the bar and lit them. Phyllis watched the flickering light brighten the dim interior. The warmth reflected on Joe's handsome face with those curious eyes still glued to hers. Two RAF officers walked in the door and up to the bar; their berets tilted at a jaunty angle. Phyllis wet her lips.

"I think Lt. Col. Lawrence was being blackmailed. I'm working on a theory that he didn't do as he was pressured to do and was turned in as a spy because of it."

Joe whistled. "Whoa! That's an interesting theory. How'd you come up with it?'"

"Well, let's not go into that now. I want you to help me do something."

"Something to help Lawrence," he prompted.

She nodded. "If it works, it could prove Lawrence didn't do anything wrong."

Joe thought for a moment. "Sure. What can I do?"

Phyllis blinked her eyes. "Just like that? You want to help me and it doesn't matter how? You don't know if it could get you in trouble or…"

"Phyllis. Honey." He reached for her hand, now chilled. "I'm a big boy and can take care of myself. At State, everyone thinks Lawrence got a raw deal and Dickie is not very popular. Do you think he had a hand in all this?"

"I'm not sure and I wouldn't want to speculate anyway. Let me get right to the point."

One of the RAF officers picked that moment to step over to their table. The colorful emblem on his beret matched his eye color and he smiled at Phyllis and Joe.

Tapping Joe's shoulder, he asked, "Don't I know you, mate?"

"Don't think so. Where do you think we met?"

"Rainbow Corner?" The officer's sunny grin grew sultry when he turned his attention to Phyllis. He tipped his beret.

"I'd like to make your acquaintance sometime, sweetheart."

Joe rose from his chair to his full height and topped the tall officer by two inches. The man threw out his hands.

"Hey! No need to get defensive. I was just making small talk."

"Make it somewhere else, mate," added Joe with a hint of sarcasm. The officer winked at Phyllis and strolled casually back to the bar.

"Cheeky devil."

"I'll say," Phyllis smirked. "Were you going to fight for my honor, Mr. Schneider?"

"Certainly, if need be, but I'd rather not rough up a member of the Allied forces if I can help it." He settled back in and picked up his glass. "Now. Where were we?" He took a pull, wiped his mouth and set the glass down.

Phyllis cleared her throat, stared at him. "I'd like you to do something for me."

He waited. "Okay." When she didn't respond immediately, he added, "Can you tell me what it is you want me to do?" Smiling, he cupped her chin. "Please?"

"You're too good to be true, Joe Schneider, and if you're a bad guy in disguise, I'm going to be really mad."

That comment broadened his smile. "I promise I'm one of the good guys."

She sucked in a deep breath. "You seem to know a lot of people and you get around."

"Yes."

"I'd like you to visit a few pubs around the Embassy and drop the word 'salamander' into conversation."

"Salamander? Like the reptile?"

"Yes, that's right. Just drop the word and see who, if anyone, reacts."

"I can tell you right now that anybody would react to the word 'salamander' because it's not a common word used in most British pubs."

"Nevertheless, I want you to try and see what kinds of reactions you get."

He focused on her solemn expression. "You're serious? You want me to say the word in casual conversation and watch how people react to what I said."

"That's correct."

"And 'salamander' means what?"

"I can't tell you that."

"Because you don't know?"

"…Because I can't tell you that."

He smiled briefly. "You could tell me but then you'd have to kill me?"

Her expression didn't waver. "This is serious stuff, Joe. If you can't or won't help me, I need to know now."

"Would you ask someone else to help you?"

"Truth?"

"Always."

"There is no one else for me to ask."

Joe leaned back in his chair and whistled softly. "This sounds like cloak and dagger stuff. Do you know what you're doing?"

"I'm…figuring it out as I go. It's been a steep learning curve."

"I'll bet."

They watched each other for another long moment. Joe opened his mouth.

"And if someone responds in some way to me? What should I do then?"

She touched his arm and whispered, "Ask them to meet you the next day at a bar we don't generally go to. Maybe something over by Bond Station.

Whoever shows up knows about salamander and could give us further information."

"Whoever shows up could be the bad guy."

"Whoever shows up could have killed Silas Reardon."

"How would you get information from him? Do you know interrogation techniques?"

"Um…no." She squirmed, looked uncomfortable. "I guess we'd have to figure it out from there or turn the guy or gal over to the military police."

"Can you tell me how you found out that 'salamander' means something covert?"

"Covert?"

"Secret."

"Well," she began, "actually no. I can't tell you anything else except that it's important."

"And could possibly help spring Lawrence from the brig."

"I sure hope so. I believe in his innocence."

He looked at her for a minute that stretched into two. "I hope you know what you're doing."

Her smile was there and gone. "So do I, Joe. So do I."

* * *

CHAPTER 33

Five pubs.

Five lousy pubs.

Joe's head hurt from the noise he'd endured making the rounds and from the five plus glasses of beer he'd had to slug down in his many conversations. Everyone he met had a sob story to tell or had hit him up for money. He couldn't count the number of times someone had plowed into him accidentally or spilled beer on his slacks. Or shoes. He reeked of stale beer and cigarettes.

Once in his flat, Joe pulled off his stinky clothes as fast as possible. His new shoes were probably wrecked and no amount of cleaning would get the smell of cigarettes out of his jacket and slacks. And that's if the dry cleaners down the street hadn't been bombed. He'd have to throw most of his clothes out.

Pulling on a fresh pair of pants, Joe went to the kitchen and poured a glass of water. He sat at the small table and drank it down with one long shallow wondering if the effort had been worth it. Trying to work the word 'salamander' into any conversation had been tough enough and every person he said it to looked at him like he'd lost his mind. It had sparked some strange conversations. One GI told him he'd eaten salamander in Australia and it had been very tasty. Much like chicken...of course.

An oldtimer from the first war went on and on about the spirit body of salamanders and that they had surprising energy fields to help the animal replicate from one generation to the next. Joe didn't know what the guy was talking about and hurried from the pub when the man finally drew breath.

At yet another dingy pub, an RAF flier announced he'd been in Iran for a while since the British and Americans were occupying forces and had bought a bracelet created there. He said it was made of iron with lovely, hand-etched artwork. When Joe asked him what that had to do with salamanders, the man shrugged and replied he thought the artist's name was something like that.

In other words, Joe had netted exactly zero on his night of cloak and dagger.

He downed another glass of water and headed for bed. What was he going to tell Phyllis? Nothing. He had nothing to tell her.

Heading towards his bed, Joe kicked his soiled jacket out of the way and heard a strange noise when it crumpled a few feet away. He walked over to pick it up, searching the inside and front pockets. In the left front pocket, Joe reached in and felt a piece of paper. Knowing he hadn't put anything in there, he excitedly pulled it out to take a look.

In a tiny cursive hand, someone had written: Meet at Nicholsons tomorrow night.

Since he'd been in five pubs and talked to dozens of men, Joe didn't have a clue who might have slipped the note in his pocket. With all the noise, sloshing ale and drunks bumping him, it could have been anyone.

He blew out a weary breath and fell into bed rereading the note. Should he mention it to Phyllis? It sounded dangerous and he didn't want her in another tricky situation. He had a funny feeling she had already been in several with her trusty companion, Lorraine.

Tugging on his blanket, Joe decided not to tell Phyllis about the note. He'd go to the pub as instructed and find out what he could. Then he'd have something more to pass on. It sounded good as he slipped into a restless sleep. Too bad it didn't turn out so well.

* * *

CHAPTER 34
May 1945

Work the next day at the State Department was tiresome. Everyone Joe spoke with was testy and irritated. The war had been going on for what seemed like forever and both Brits and Americans would be thrilled if it were finally over.

Word was out that the Soviet offensive had captured Budapest after a two-month siege. US troops had crossed the Rhine River at Remagen and Berlin was encircled by the Soviets. Joe would have thought news this good would have brightened a few spirits, but nothing really changed for the everyday Londoner or American living there. Blackout conditions still existed with the occasional buzz bomb creating havoc. In addition, V-2 bombs were still destroying sections of London but in a sneakier way: buzz bombs could be heard before they landed, not so with the V-2. This destruction was more calculated, more sophisticated with pinpoint accuracy.

Besides pubs and gatherings in private homes, there wasn't a great deal for the average Londoner to do. If money wasn't tight, which it usually was, Madame Tussaud's Wax Museum was open near Baker Street Station but it was mainly Americans who visited. Joe knew the girls at Seven Addison Bridge Place went into Ipswich sometimes to party with the GIs at the P51 Mustang fighter base.

Buckingham Palace was sooty, gloomy and looked as neglected as the rest of London. The National Gallery in Trafalgar Square had long queues waiting to get in on Picture of the Month day. Only one famous painting could be viewed at a time since the entire collection had been removed for safekeeping outside of town. The Gallery's director brought in one painting a month and if bombs weren't flying, Londoners went to see it. Masterpieces were more prized when there were so few of them to see.

An occasional musical concert was held in a basement shelter, but Rainbow Corner had closed so GIs on leave flocked to the Savoy, Claridge's and the Ritz to hobnob with the rich and famous for a few frothy hours. Churches functioned the best they could, if their buildings were still standing and the occasional movie was shown at a local theater, if a film could be wrangled from somewhere. Moviegoers watched anything that was shown and generally found out what movie was playing when they arrived that evening.

Joe went about his usual workday responsibilities, but brightened considerably when the day was done. His friend Henry asked him to grab a pint so they ended up at Blue Anchor a few streets over.

"Try not to get sloshed tonight, Henry."

"What's it to you?"

Joe glared at him. "Who do you think got you home that last time? Do you even remember being here?"

Henry glanced around the pub. Only a few patrons sat on stools next to the counter. "Nah. Not really." He angled his head towards the bar. "I remember that crazy Scot being a jerk though."

"How so?"

"Lorraine and I were having a few laughs when he tried to throw me out...I think." He pouted, picked up his glass for a long drink.

Joe laughed. "Your memory's a little faulty, my good man."

"How would you know?"

"Because...I walked in just in time to see you hunched over the table, Lorraine trying to move you and Malcolm getting pissed. He's dated her a few times, you know, and Scots are particular with their women."

Henry snorted in his beer. "Right. I haven't met a Scot yet who dated just one girl at a time. I've seen him out and about with other women."

"Well, me too, but don't tell him that." Joe's smile stretched across his face. "We'll never get another drink in this place."

"No loss. The roof's caving in anyway. After that last bomb, I thought it was a goner and good riddance."

"Harsh, man," Joe chuckled. He looked across the pub and signaled another round to Malcolm. "Let's have one for the road."

"What's the hurry?"

"Places to go, people to see."

Henry drained his beer. "What places? What people?"

"Secret State Department business," he lied.

"After hours?"

Joe shook his head, picked up his glass to make room for the fresh ale Malcolm was bringing over. "Sorry. Can't talk about it. Maybe someday but not tonight."

The bartender plunked two glasses in front of Joe and Henry spilling some beer on the table. He mumbled something under his breath and stepped away.

"What's that you say?" Joe cupped his ear. "Can't hear you."

"I said," announced Malcolm loudly, "that I'm going off duty so settle up with Spence."

"Oh sure. Sure thing," Joe said to Malcolm's retreating back.

"What crawled up his butt?"

"Maybe he's got a hot date."

"Better not be with Lorraine."

"Why not? You seein' her tonight?"

"Well, no," Henry admitted, "but I'm callin' her later, so it would be nice if she was at home to get my call."

Joe tried not to smirk. "When have you ever heard of Lorraine being home?"

Henry blushed. "Okay, okay. She's a butterfly, that one."

"And not settling down anytime soon."

161

Henry threw out his hands. "Hey! Who said anything about settling down?"

"Drink up. I have to go soon."

"...Go ahead and take off if you need to."

"You'll be all right?"

"Yeah," he laughed, "but thanks for the concern." Joe reached for his wallet. "No, no. I've got this. I owe you—apparently."

"Thanks." Joe emptied his glass with a long swallow and rose. "See you tomorrow."

"Tomorrow."

But tomorrow was promised to no man as Joe set off across town for his rendezvous, a meeting with the unknown. He hoped it wouldn't be accompanied by its ally: danger.

* * *

CHAPTER 35

Darkness fell hard in London these days. The city was a mish-mash of crumpled buildings, toppled statuary and destroyed streets. It was such a dichotomy; two streets and around the corner from the Blue Anchor, old brick buildings stood together like sentries protecting people inside and around. Complete destruction in one section of town belied the relative peace of the next section over. Paint peeling from storefronts looked as if they were shedding their skin. Shedding the war perhaps.

Joe mused as he walked along, minding that his torch never shone upward, that he had given up a complacent life in the States to become some kind of spook in war-ravaged London. He felt slightly conspicuous with his wool overcoat, semi-new shoes and fedora when children ran past him laughing, heading for home. He slogged through puddles from the last rain but was wound up like a prizefighter raring to go.

Turning a corner, he saw the dilapidated sign reading *Nicholson's*. Yeah, this was the place to meet Mr. Big from instructions on the note in his pocket. What was he planning to do with that? Use it like a get-in-free ticket? Joe's fingers clasped the note more for a semblance of calm, a reminder of what he was doing, why he was here.

It was for Phyllis.

And yet it was for a higher purpose—there was a spy to be caught and he wanted to help her do just that. If he could contribute anything to winning the war against Germany, it could very well be this. Joe was prepared to do whatever it took to solve this puzzle and his hand released the note to gently stroke the sleek revolver next to it in his overcoat pocket.

The tumbledown awning of the pub was in front of him; Joe drew in a deep breath and stepped in.

The women at Seven Addison Bridge Place were having some fun. Good smells from the casserole cooking in the oven warmed the small kitchen along with the presence of the bubbly young women. In the midst of laughter, Doris twirled a hand towel and smacked Norma with it while chasing her behind Phyllis.

"Hey! Cut that out!"

"Sparky told me you went out with Dave."

"So? We all go out with Dave."

Doris' hands were on her waist. "Well, he's mine!"

"Since when?" Phyllis snickered. "Everyone here has been on a date with him. I thought he was…interchangeable."

"Well…well, I…" Doris sputtered. "We were getting serious."

Mildred and Mrs. Stewart joined Phyllis and Norma for a heartfelt laugh at Doris' flabbergasted face.

"Oh, honey, you're kidding yourself if you think that guy wants to settle down." Norma peeked around Phyllis who was attempting to cut slices of cheese to go with the casserole. Pretty Norma blinked sympathetic eyes at Doris' woebegone expression. Suddenly, tiny Mrs. Stewart was by her side reaching up to pat Doris's shoulder and Mildred was holding her hand.

"Tsk, tsk," murmured Mrs. Stewart. "Mustn't fall for one of these fliers, hon. You know they're all just havin' a bit of fun."

Mildred nodded. "That's right. The war could be over soon and we'll all head in opposite directions, most likely."

Silence fell around the kitchen until Phyllis resumed scraping the mold off the cheese. Norma's head swung round to peer at Phyllis' handiwork. Her nose scrunched and she held her breath.

"Where did you get that cheese, Phyllis?"

164

"It's goat cheese, Norma. Mrs. Stewart got it from her friend Edna who lives out of town. She's got a few goats and makes this incredible cheese."

"Yeah," breathed Mildred. "It *is* a little stinky, Phyl. Maybe we should open a window."

"No open windows, girls! You know what happened the last time we opened a window."

"Mrs. Stewart, it's hot in here and now it's smelly too. We haven't had a buzz bomb in a week. Please?" pleaded Doris with threaded fingers like she was offering up a prayer to the wind gods.

"Nope and that's final." Mrs. Stewart glanced around the kitchen. "And where's your partner in crime, Phyllis? Why isn't she helping you with dinner? It's not like her to miss a meal."

The girls giggled appreciatively until Phyllis quieted them down with a stern look.

"I'm not sure, to tell you the truth." She looked at the clock on the wall. "She should be here by now, that's true."

The girls took plates and glasses out of the cupboard to begin setting the table in the dining room. Phyllis finished slicing the cheese and checked the casserole as Mrs. Stewart headed back to her flat. Just as Phyllis started to pull the dish out of the oven, she heard the phone ring in the parlor and Mrs. Stewart answered it.

"Hello? Who is it? We're about to have supper…Uh-huh…sure. Let me call her. Phyllis? Come get this phone. It's Lorraine for you!"

Her shout brought all the girls clamoring to the phone, talking and giggling. Phyllis picked up the receiver. "Hello? Lorraine?" She tried to shush the girls and held up a hand for quiet. "Shh! I can't hear her."

"Move along, girls. Let Phyllis have some privacy for her very short call." She narrowed her eyes at Phyllis who nodded briskly. When it was quiet, Phyllis tried again. "Lorraine?"

"Phyllis?"

"Yes, it's me."

Pause. "Is…anyone else listening?"

What? "No. No one. Where are you?"

Phyllis heard her whispering to someone.

"I'm in Canning Town."

"Canning Town? Clear out in West Ham? Oh, sweetie. What in the world are you doing way out there?"

"I need you to pick me up."

Phyllis' eyebrows shot into her hairline. "Are you kidding me? That's miles from here and it'll take forever on the tube—probably three train changes at least."

"Please, Phyllis. I need you to do this."

Her voice sounded shaky and not at all like her. Lorraine was super confident and so sure of herself that Phyllis thought nothing could crack her confidence, but she didn't sound so very confident now. In fact, she sounded panicky.

"Okay, okay. Tell me where you are."

"I'm at the..." she cleared her throat, "Canning Town tube station. I'll be waiting."

"And I'll be waiting for an explanation. Why can't you just get on the tube and come home?"

"Ah...no, I can't...do that. I need you to come here."

"All right, but can you at least tell me why you're there?"

"Don't ask me any more questions, Phyl. Just come get me..." She broke off when someone spoke to her. "...And come alone."

"Okay. I'll be there as soon as I can."

Phyllis hung up the receiver wondering what was wrong with her friend. She'd never heard her scared before and there was no good reason whatsoever to be in that destroyed section of the East End. With all the bombings in that area, she'd heard there were few habitable buildings left and most of the population had gotten out if they could. Roving gangs and crime were the mainstays now.

Shaking her head, Phyllis went upstairs for her coat and hat. As she skipped downstairs, Mrs. Stewart caught her before she opened the front door.

"Where are you going, Phyllis? It's suppertime. We're all about to sit down and eat, remember? You cooked it!"

"Yes, yes, Mrs. Stewart. I know but Lorraine wants me to come get her."

"Why can't she get here herself?"

"I...I'm not sure, but I need to go." She stepped towards the door but Mrs. Stewart grabbed her arm again.

"I don't like the sound of this, missy. Where's that handsome boyfriend of yours? Couldn't he at least go with you?"

"Joe! Yes! Good idea." Phyllis hurried to the phone and dialed his number. After counting ten rings, she hung up.

"He's not home?"

"No. I can't think where he might be." But then she remembered what she had asked him to do and it showed on her face. Mrs. Stewart was right there.

"You know where he is, don't you?"

Phyllis wrung her hands. "I have a...pretty good idea, Mrs. Stewart, but it doesn't change the fact that I can't get ahold of him. Let me go."

She released Phyllis' arm with reluctance. "I don't like you heading off somewhere at night without telling me where you're going."

"I can't. Honestly."

"Phyllis? What's happening? Aren't we going to eat?" Norma called from the dining room and when Mrs. Stewart turned to respond, Phyllis slipped out the door.

"Hey!" she called out watching Phyllis run toward the train station. "Come back here!" Her words fell on deaf ears and she closed the door behind her.

"This night isn't going to have a pretty ending, I just know it."

* * *

CHAPTER 36

"She's not here, Joe. We don't know where she went," pouted Norma.

An irritated Doris interrupted. "Yes, we were sitting down to eat a supper she cooked and Mrs. Stewart said she just up and left."

"She just left?" His brows furrowed deeply. "Without telling anyone where she was going?" He glanced out the parlor window. "But it'll be dark soon."

"We know it, Joe. Want to join us?" cooed Mildred. "There's still some casserole left and a few slices of smelly goat cheese."

Joe's brief smile faded. "Thanks, ladies, but I need to find her. Where's Mrs. Stewart?"

"Back in her flat. The cheese chased her away."

"I can imagine. See you."

"Bye, Joe." Mildred, Doris and Norma waved at him as he walked towards the front door. Mrs. Stewart came out to meet him.

"I heard all that, Mr. Schneider. Just where were you earlier when Phyllis tried to reach you?" The tiny landlady stood on tiptoes to shake a finger in Joe's confused face.

"I was…elsewhere, Mrs. Stewart. Now tell me why she left."

"She got a phone call, a curious call."

"From whom?"

"Lorraine, that's who."

Was he going to have to drag it out of her?

"Please, Mrs. Stewart. Tell me what's going on."

"I'm sure I don't know. Do you think I'm some kind of snoop?"

Not touching that one.

"What can you tell me?"

Mrs. Stewart scratched her chin and her eyes slid to the phone. "All right. Phyllis seems to trust you, so I guess I will." She folded her arms across her chest. "Lorraine called and asked her to come get her."

"Where?"

"Canning Town tube station."

He blinked in total surprise. "You're kidding! That place must be falling down by now."

"That's what I heard Phyllis say to Lorraine, but apparently she insisted that was where she was."

"And Phyllis should pick her up?" Mrs. Stewart nodded. "Trains still go to that area. Why couldn't she just get on a train by herself?"

"Don't know but it sounds pretty fishy to me, Mr. Schneider. So…"

"So?"

"So what are you still doing talking to me? Go get our girl."

Joe tensely nodded, hurried to the door and opened it when Mildred and Doris came rushing in, Norma right behind them, their faces ablaze with happiness.

"Joe! Mrs. Stewart! Did you hear? Did you hear?"

"Hear what?"

They were jumping up and down, clapping their hands and screaming.

"Girls! Quiet down now. That's not dignified behavior with Mr. Schneider here."

"Well, he needs to hear this too!" exclaimed Norma.

"Hear what?" asked Joe. Looking from one exuberant face to another, he knew something fantastic had happened.

"Hitler's dead!" they all screamed at once. Clapping and shrieking, the girls began dancing around the entryway. Joe had to step out of the way to stay out of their improvised conga line. He grabbed Norma's shoulders, swung her around to face him.

"Where did you hear this?"

169

"We just heard it on the BBC! Someone announced that Hitler had been killed at the Reich Chancery in Berlin," said Doris with a wide-eyed expression.

"And," added Mildred, "he had appointed Grand Admiral Doenitz as his successor."

Joe gazed at the scene before him like he was having an out-of-body experience. He felt himself hovering overhead looking down at the dancing girls. It was too much to even hope for, much less believe! Before he could get too excited however, he whistled for quiet. "Listen. That's wonderful news, of course, but we've got an immediate problem—Phyllis and Lorraine. I'm going to Canning Town to find them." He singled out Mrs. Stewart. "If we're not back in two hours, call the police."

Her mouth dropped open. "Really? Do you think it's as bad as all that?"

"I do." He locked eyes with the feisty woman whose chin jutted out defensively. Relenting, she nodded once.

"Then go!" she commanded pointing a finger at the front door. He smiled and hurried out. "And tell her that crabby sister of hers called again!"

* * *

170

CHAPTER 37

What a night! Sitting dejectedly on the train, Joe felt like he was riding a roller coaster swerving wildly out of control.

After leaving Henry, he'd gone to Nicholson's, a seedy pub a few streets over from the Embassy. He'd waited for over an hour and no one approached him at all! What was going on? Why had someone slipped a note in his pocket to meet with him when no one showed up? The more he thought about it, the more he decided that the pub was an obvious ruse. Whoever it was wanted him to be in one place out of the way, perhaps. And if that were the case, did they want him out of the way for a sinister reason?

Those dire thoughts and more clouded his mind as he watched the ruins of London speed by. It took a few train changes to leave central London and head for the East End, but it afforded him a good look at the city in all its horrifying glory.

The remnants of a once popular church lay in rubble all over an empty street. Only a tall spire remained pointing high into a sky everyone looked at now, anticipating the next bomb. Boards, shards, glass and bricks lay in piles while dark figures stood looking intently at the devastation. Perhaps they were members of the congregation at one time and were wondering where they could go now to pray for their ever-lasting souls. To baptize their children. To find a crumb of fleeting normalcy.

Joe swung his head in another direction to look out at the scene rushing by from the window across the aisle. Another traveler turned to look with him like they were watching a movie, something unreal—a fictionalized world in another dimension. Sections of West Ham going by were missing. The picture was oddly incomplete with buildings cut strangely in half, smoke rising from fires, yet with trucks driving along unhurriedly going about business as usual. Even though it was dusk, he saw people riding on bicycles and women pushing babies in prams in haphazard motion to avoid the destroyed parts of the street. If he hadn't seen it with his own eyes, it would have been too much fantasy to be believed.

He slumped in his seat and closed his eyes, willing the war to be over so the historic city could rise again. Phyllis' image was painted on the inside of his eyelids and he wished with all his heart she would be alive when he got there. But with his tradecraft training, he knew there was a possibility she was dead. Lorraine too. Things had gotten out of control and it could all end so very badly.

* * *

CHAPTER 38

Phyllis headed for the Canning Town tube station. What a joke. The tube wasn't running in this section of town and she'd had to catch two different trains to get this far. Shining her flashlight around the broken sidewalk trying hard not to fall, she missed the bobby who would scold her for shining her torch too high. She missed seeing anyone at all. There were occasional scary shadows looming on walls that had once been part of an apartment building or café, but the good times had definitely left this section of London. The shadows sometimes turned out to be stray dogs, which could be even more problematic.

She quickened her sluggish pace.

Stumbling along, Phyllis couldn't imagine what Lorraine was doing way out here and at this time of night. She shivered, clutching her coat more tightly, and straightened her hat tipping dangerously to one side. Anxiety and nerves kept her moving briskly as her jumbled thoughts auditioned for most important. Stepping lightly, she heard an unusual sound and froze. Phyllis glanced anxiously about hoping for something but praying for nothing. She was ill equipped to fight off a robber or attacking animal being armed with only a pencil in her purse and her Daughters of the American Revolution hatpin.

Nothing untoward moved from the shadows, so she took a new step, then another…listening all the while for a sound that never came. Her echoing footsteps kept her company but the flashlight was beginning to sputter. Oh no! She had forgotten to put in fresh batteries yesterday like she'd meant to. Her heart began beating faster as the level of adrenaline in her body kicked up a notch.

With spooky shadows on bombed out buildings and a flashlight on the wane, Phyllis suddenly realized that she was lost. She'd never been to Canning Town, but someone on the train had told her where to go to find the disused tube station. In the dark, she'd gotten turned around. Her anxiety kicked into overdrive, so she squatted for a moment to catch her breath. She cupped hands around her mouth to fight off a panic attack and breathed as normally as her frantic brain would allow her. Feeling light-headed, Phyllis fought to regain her composure. When she felt better, she stood and began walking again. Her light reflected off a still standing street sign and it was a rush of relief to realize she was heading in the right direction. With a little more confidence, she brushed curly hair from her eyes and straightened her posture.

She could do this.

Remnants of a large sign reading Station alerted Phyllis that she'd reached the end of her journey. But looking in every direction, she couldn't for the life of her see anyone around. The place resembled the surface of the moon, not an old town established back when the Romans roamed the area. Leaving wasn't an option because this was where Lorraine was supposed to be, but had someone sent her on a wild goose chase? And for what possible reason? She raced through her limited options not settling on a satisfying one when she heard a woman's faint cry.

Phyllis' head automatically swerved in that direction. When her light conked out, only the partial moon gave light to those unlucky enough to be at this location at this given moment. She heard nothing more until…two figures moved from behind a brick wall by the sign. When they moved closer, she recognized her friend walking in front. Lorraine's pale hair had tumbled into a tangled mess on her shoulders. She was shivering, probably because she had no coat and her thin dress was ripped down the skirt. Phyllis wanted to grab Lorraine and run when she saw the blood on her face and along one arm. The expression on her face was that of abject terror.

In the moonlight, she squinted her eyes trying to see who was behind Lorraine. A man with light hair and a beard?

"Lorraine? Are you all right?"

When she didn't answer but stood trembling, Phyllis called out to the man. "Why are her hands tied and just what do you want?"

Noticing the gun in his hand, Phyllis knew the hatpin would be of no use, the pencil even less.

It hit her like a bucket of cold water. "Malcolm? What the hell do you think you're doing?"

He poked Lorraine in the back making her flinch, but got her stepping forward. She tripped on debris at her feet and Phyllis lurched forward to help her.

"Stand back!" Malcolm pointed the gun at Phyllis.

She took a deep breath and leveled an icy stare his way.

"I'll repeat my question: what are you doing? What do you want?"

"That's two questions, lassie."

"Quit being cute, Malcolm. It doesn't suit you." That wiped the smile off his face. The look replacing it was downright scary.

"Since I'm in charge of this here situation, you'd best be nicer."

She and Lorraine stared at each other while waiting for Malcolm's next move. When nothing came and feeling out of moves herself, Phyllis decided she had nothing to lose. "You killed Silas Reardon."

He shook his head. "Just had to get involved, didn't ya? It wasn't a smart thing to do and you've always seemed like a smart girl. Except hanging out with this wild one." He twisted a lock of Lorraine's hair between stubby fingers. "She's been a right pistol."

"I can see that you had to slap her around. So you're not a nice man after all."

"Never said I was."

"Reardon?" she persisted.

"He got greedy."

"How?"

Malcolm poked Lorraine in the back again forcing her to take another step. When Phyllis moved too, he pointed the pistol at her.

"Back up. Not so close." He looked at Phyllis with the hardened eyes of a predator beginning his attack. "I guess I can tell you some. It's not like you're gonna run away and tell somebody." He chuckled softly at his own joke.

Phyllis kept quiet dreading the words to come, yet knowing they would be freeing, momentarily at least.

"He wanted more."

"You were selling secrets?"

"Yeah, to the highest bidder, mostly Germans but to the Russians too."

"Big market for left over tanks and guns?"

He smiled a wolfish grin. "I knew you were the smart one. The black market is buying everything not nailed down and we've made a killing already."

"So to speak," she mumbled. When he looked at her curiously, she said louder, "But Silas wanted more."

"Yes, there was plenty for both of us but he upped his end."

"So you killed him."

He cocked his head, laid a hand on Lorraine's shoulder causing her terrified eyes to widen. "Actually, it was an accident."

"You met in the vault," Phyllis prompted.

"Very good. We always met in the vault. For years now we've met in the vault."

"For years?"

He nodded. "Lawrence wouldn't let anyone down there so it was a perfect place."

"You framed him, right? Whatever did he do to you?"

"He discovered us one night and threatened to expose us both. Before he had the chance, Silas planted some sensitive material on him and leaked it to the FBI."

Something wasn't adding up. Phyllis took a step forward.

"Back up, sister. I wouldn't want to shoot your girlfriend here."

176

"Silas must not have had much use for Lawrence."

"He wanted the job after Bradley retired. When Reardon was passed over, he got mad and decided to make some money instead. He was drinkin' in the pub one night and we started talkin'. Before long, we were in business together." Malcolm looked around at the desolate area. "He'll go down for everything now because I'm out of here tonight."

"You're leaving town?"

"Just tyin' up loose threads."

"And us? Are we those loose threads you so quaintly described?"

His grin was wicked. "You girls have been in the way long enough. I knew you were getting close but Lorraine's mouth was a bit too closed. I tried to find out what she knew and she just had to be a tosser."

Malcolm raised his pistol before cocking it. "Bye, girls. It's been fun." Just as he aimed at Lorraine's back, the ground around them shook hard enough to knock everyone off their feet. A concussive wave of sound sent their bodies flying through the air coming to rest in the rubble of the destroyed station.

Phyllis landed hard with rocks jammed in her back and legs and broken glass working its way into an arm. When her mind stopped rockin' and rollin', her first clear thought was to thank the V-2 bomb that was supposed to have killed them. Maybe it saved her and Lorraine instead. She shook her head attempting to clear the haze both physically and mentally, then took a good look around. When the dust lifted, Lorraine was lying several feet away, not moving at all. Malcolm was closer and had awakened when Phyllis did; they exchanged surprised glances that bordered on shock.

She propped up on one elbow and noticed his hands were empty.

Where was the gun?

They saw it at the same time and looked from the gun laying between them to each other. There was a split second before frozen inactivity changed to furious activity as Phyllis and Malcolm scrambled desperately towards the gun. Glass cut into her leg when she moved tearing a cry from tight lips. Malcolm grunted from his own problems and they crashed into one another falling into a heap as they struggled for control of the weapon.

Lying on her stomach, she got her hands on it first, but Malcolm wrestled it away. He leaned back aiming clumsily and shot at Phyllis twice; one bullet wildly pinged off something behind her, but the other grazed her arm. The bite of pain pinched hard causing her to cry out. Still she lurched forward to make another desperate grab for him. Just as he aimed at her again, another shot rang out and Malcolm slumped over on his side. Phyllis fell back exhausted and bleeding. She lay as still as possible counting her choppy breaths, so happy to be alive when a familiar face loomed overhead.

He crouched down beside her with a big smile and a bigger revolver.

"Hi, sweetheart. Having a bad day?"

Her face crumbled with tears falling hard and fast. Joe scooped her up in his arms where she sobbed with abandon. Pushing away after a few therapeutic minutes, Phyllis fished the hanky out of her coat pocket to noisily blow her nose. Joe carefully prodded her arm checking out her wound.

"I…I thought I was a…goner," she warbled.

"Don't I know it. Sure didn't look good from where I was standing."

"Lorraine!"

"Come on. Let's get her."

Joe pulled Phyllis to unsteady feet and held onto her as they moved cautiously to where Lorraine had fallen. They picked rocks and debris off her until she stirred. Phyllis brushed dusty hair from her face and they sat her up. With a groggy expression, she blinked rapidly.

"What happened? One minute Malcolm was going to shoot me and the next, I wake up with you two clowns staring at me."

Phyllis gathered Lorraine in her arms, crying softly. Lorraine broke down too, so Joe gave them a private moment. He climbed over rocks and bricks to check Malcolm and retrieve his gun. When Lorraine looked down at Phyllis' arm, she gasped. A hand flew to her mouth.

"You've been shot!"

"Come on, girls. We need to get out of here. I've got to get you both to the nearest hospital and I need to call this in, have someone pick up the body."

As he wrapped his overcoat around Lorraine and used her hanky to tie a tourniquet on Phyllis' wounded arm, she watched him with narrowing eyes.

"You need to call this in? To the State Department?"

He grinned sheepishly. "I've got a taxi waiting the next street over. Let's get moving."

"Joe…"

"Do we have to do this now?"

"Yes."

He sighed deeply. "This goes nowhere, right?" The look he gave Phyllis and then Lorraine was stern. When they nodded, he turned to Phyllis. "I'm MI5, honey."

Somehow she wasn't too surprised. "Were you sent in by the government to investigate Lawrence?"

"Yes, but doing so, I stumbled into the middle of a war profiteering scheme." He took her hand. "And you." Bringing her hand to his lips, he kissed it gently.

"So was I just part of the scenery?"

"No, of course not."

"Did you use me, Joe?"

He glanced to Lorraine for help. When she nodded encouragement, he continued. "Maybe it started that way, Phyllis, but it sure didn't end like that. Somewhere along the line, I did the unthinkable for an agent and fell for my subject."

"So you…you're saying that you love me?"

179

"Yes, in those very words. I'm in love with you." He pecked her lips. "Now can we get you to a hospital? You're bleeding all over your coat."

Phyllis' face lit up. She turned to Lorraine. "He loves me."

"Of course, he does, you idiot. Now can we go?"

Once they were in the taxi heading for the hospital, Lorraine fell asleep. Phyllis burrowed into Joe's side with his arm wrapped tightly around her.

"How did you know where we were?"

"Mrs. Stewart overheard your phone conversation with Lorraine and put two and two together."

"Of course. Nosy Mrs. Stewart. Thank God for nosy Mrs. Stewart."

"She really does know everything that goes on in that house."

"Very true."

Phyllis yawned, quieted for a few minutes. Joe kissed her cheek.

"Sleep if you can."

She peered up into his face. "What about that woman at the train station?"

"What woman?"

When she didn't respond, Joe laughed. "Oh, I get it. You had someone follow me when we first met to see if I was on the level."

"Well, you weren't."

"Okay." Blushing, he kissed her again. "Maybe not then, but I met a contact for information, that's all. That was pretty smart of you to check me out too."

"I knew I was going to be in trouble sooner or later and wondered if I could count on you."

"Did that encounter at the station deter you from trusting me?"

"Lorraine didn't trust you but..." she smiled, "any man who kisses like you do can't be all bad."

"Thank you."

"So tell me again that I'm not just a source."

"Far from it."

"Prove it."

"I intend to." Joe raised her chin with a finger and pressed his lips to hers for a lingering kiss. They broke apart unwillingly when the taxi driver interrupted.

"Hey mister! We're at the hospital."

* * *

CHAPTER 39
May 8, 1945

With a day off, Joe and Phyllis visited a movie theater in downtown London on May 8 to see *Spellbound,* the new Alfred Hitchcock movie. Suspense was mastered once again by the famed director as Ingrid Bergman played a charming psychiatrist carrying her attentions a little too far towards Gregory Peck, a victim of amnesia. But the movie was entertaining to the happy couple holding hands throughout and darting loving glances at one another from time to time. When they left the theater, an incredible sight met their unbelieving eyes.

All of London was out celebrating!

Germany had surrendered to the Allied Forces on May 7, but German soldiers laid down their weapons on May 8, officially Victory in Europe Day or V-E Day. They walked up to Piccadilly Circus and watched people climbing telephone poles to see around them better. Thousands crowded the streets waving American and British flags. If you continued looking, there were a few flags of other nations involved with the Allies. It seemed that the whole of London was out waving flags, eagerly kissing pretty young women or dancing a quick jitterbug with whoever was handy. Colorful paper littered the streets with cars honking and people singing or screeching at the top of their lungs.

People were jammed in tightly and wherever there was room on the side streets, the crowd was dancing in conga chains. Joe and Phyllis bought a souvenir featuring British and American flags. Phyllis heard from a boisterous RAF officer that England would have three days of celebration with Prime Minister Churchill waving to crowds and giving broadcasts. Churches and cathedrals would ring bells and the BBC would be broadcasting international recording stars and celebrities. From a woman about to climb a phone pole, Joe learned that on Sunday, May 10, a service of thanksgiving would be held at Westminster Abbey and attended by veterans, their families, members of the Royal Family and representatives of allied nations who fought alongside Britain in the harrowing conflict.

It was almost too much to take in!

They fought their way through the friendly crowd back to Seven Addison Bridge Place and hoped to find some peace and quiet, but that's not what they found upon arrival. Mrs. Stewart had opened her row house up to anyone who wanted to come in and stretched her arms wide to welcome Phyllis and Joe. Perhaps it was an unofficial open house, but everyone they knew dropped in to share in the celebration and even many people they didn't know showed up. All were welcome on this momentous occasion!

After a few hours, Phyllis looked around but couldn't find Mrs. Stewart. Knowing the diminutive landlady as she did, Phyllis wasn't surprised to find her back in her flat. She was gazing fondly at a photo above her fireplace. In all the time she'd known her, Phyllis had never, ever seen her looking so incredibly happy.

Grouchy, yes.

Angry, yes.

But deliriously happy? No.

"Phyllis! Come in!" She'd never welcomed any of the girls she rented to at the row house into her private domain. It was sacred territory they never dared venture into. But seeing Phyllis through the glass in her door, she motioned for her to come in.

"Sit down, sit down! Please! Have a seat in my chair." Mrs. Stewart waved her to a threadbare chair with springs showing through the nearly transparent material. When Phyllis started to sit, Mrs. Stewart stopped her.

"Wait. Use this cushion. It'll help. How's the arm?" An unexpected twinkle in the tiny woman's eye had Phyllis nearly dumbfounded.

"It's good, thank you. It was just a flesh wound really." A beat passed. "I wanted to check on you…"

"Yes, yes." Mrs. Stewart clicked her tongue, pushed Phyllis into the chair and shoved a framed photo into her hands. "Look at this."

It was an official picture of a young man wearing a British Army uniform.

"He's very handsome." She looked up. "Who is he?"

A quiet serenity settled on the woman's features. Moisture pooled in her eyes and she had to swallow several times before she could speak.

"That's my son, Frederick. He was only twenty when he enlisted and I haven't seen him for three years."

"Do you know where he is now?"

She shook her head, tears fell on pale cheeks. "Last I heard from the War Department was that he had been captured and was in a prison camp somewhere in Germany."

Phyllis' hand flew to her mouth. "Oh, my! I can't imagine how you've been coping, Mrs. Stewart."

The little landlady smiled. "Having you girls here has been the light in my life for as long as I've known you." She sat down across from Phyllis on the couch and took the picture. Cradling it lovingly in her arms, she looked up with eyes full of tears.

"I've lived through the Blitz, the buzz bombs and the V-2 bombs. I've endured the shortages and the blackouts. My house has been bombed, but I'm still here." She huskily cleared her throat. "And here I will remain until my boy comes back to me."

In tears herself, Phyllis reached over to take her small hand. "It's been an honor to live here with you, Mrs. Stewart. I know you'll see Frederick very soon now."

She squeezed Phyllis' hand and smiled. "Thank you." Fishing a hanky from her apron, she angled her head towards the door. "Go on with you now. Go back to the party."

"Will you rejoin us?"

"Sure, sure. Very soon. I just needed a moment alone."

"I'm sorry I intruded."

"Oh no, Phyllis. You've never been an intrusion. You're a lovely young woman, no matter what that cranky sister of yours says."

At that they both smiled. Phyllis rose.

"I'll see you later then."

"Later…"

Phyllis went back out to the party, but there were fewer people, less shrieking and more contented faces. Lorraine, Mildred, Norma and Doris were sitting quietly in the parlor with a few of their flier friends from the base at Ipswich. Sparky, Dave and Roger sat on one side with Cliff and Max sandwiched between Norma and Doris. Henry and Joe stood to one side and Joe broke away to give Phyllis a hug when she rejoined the group.

"Missed you."

"I…had a sweet talk with Mrs. Stewart."

"Mrs. Stewart? Sweet?"

Phyllis smiled into his jacket. Looking up into his handsome face, she almost sighed. "I'll tell you about it someday."

"I'm looking forward to it."

She glanced around at faces she knew well and loved. They'd all been through the last year of the war together and the bonds created she knew would last a lifetime.

"Why the long faces? This is supposed to be a party!"

"It is, Phyl, sure," began Sparky. "But we're not done, remember."

"Yeah, Sparky's right." Dave twirled the glass in his hand. "As Americans we have to be conscious of the fact there's another war to be won."

"True," added Lorraine solemnly. "Our boys are still fighting in the Pacific."

"Last we heard about was the battle in Okinawa."

"That settles it then," Roger stood and raised his glass. "Here's to victory in the Pacific."

Everyone rose and toasted with him. "To victory in the Pacific."

After drinking their glasses dry, people began to leave. Everyone exchanged heartfelt hugs, kisses on moist cheeks and pats on the back. Henry and Joe shook hands, then Henry walked over to be with Lorraine. He gave her a hug and whispered in her ear. Phyllis watched for a moment, before turning back to the cute guy watching her with a wide grin and sparkling eyes. She grabbed hold of his lapels and leaned in close.

"I'm exhausted, Joe."

"Stay with me tonight, honey."

She shook her head. "Lorraine needs me and so does Mrs. Stewart, truth be told."

"Really?"

"Really."

"Okay, then. Tomorrow night."

Her smile was sly. "Hmm..." She tapped her chin. "Think I should?"

"Yes, honey." Joe brushed her lips for a sweet kiss that went on and on.

"Maybe I should," she whispered.

She walked him to the door where he kissed her again and squeezed her hand. "I'll call you."

Henry followed him out leaving Lorraine and Phyllis smiling at one another. Norma, Mildred and Doris had already left for their bedrooms and the house was as still as unmoving water.

"Life is good, isn't it, Lorraine?"

"I'll say."

"So," Phyllis arched a playful brow, "...it's Henry, is it?"

186

Lorraine shrugged, grinned saucily. "Maybe. I'll see how I feel tomorrow."

"Silly girl. He's crazy about you."

"Joe's pretty crazy about you too."

"I know. He's a keeper."

"He saved our collective asses, Phyl. He's more than a keeper: he's a life saver."

"And he's MI5."

"So? It's not a contagious disease." Before Phyllis could respond, Lorraine held up a hand. "No more tonight. This has been a wonderful day with wonderful friends and we're going to leave it on a wonderful note. All right?"

"Wonderful."

They laughed as they headed upstairs together, separated at the top of the staircase and waved as they went to their respective bedrooms.

"To a wonderful tomorrow."

"I agree. Good night."

* * *

CHAPTER 40

Work the following week was light, almost fluffy with Embassy employees being exceedingly cordial to one another. Martha brought Phyllis a blooming plant for her desk and all the girls in the steno pool chattered constantly getting very little work done. Lunch in the Officers' Mess offered a rare treat on the menu: oranges! Phyllis hadn't seen an orange in months and wondered where the food service people had managed to find them.

Dickie invited everyone to a special lunch on Wednesday. Phyllis had never seen him smile so much and by Wednesday morning, he was positively giddy. She'd asked him what was going on, but he smugly shook his head telling her she would have to wait like everyone else. And since he was so prolific this week, she had little time for idle curiosity anyway. She wore out the ribbon in her typewriter and had to return to that hideous supply closet for another. This time she had Lorraine stand at the door while she dashed in and out in record time getting what she needed.

At noon, the girls filed into the cavernous Officers' Mess on the first floor. A large room to be sure with space on balconies for more tables and chairs if needed. Today, proud members of the American Embassy occupied nearly every seat in the house. Service staff waited on them, which was a rare occurrence. Members of the military police, the FBI and a few Army generals were sprinkled among the gathering causing much speculation about what Dickie was going to say.

Lorraine and Phyllis, sitting with other women from the pool, made wild guesses. Everything from the war in the Pacific being over to Eleanor Roosevelt making a surprise visit was discussed thoroughly and discarded. No one knew what was happening, but were confused as to why Phyllis, Dickie's secretary, didn't know. She shrugged and had no answers.

By the time coffee and dessert were offered, Major Richard Simpson walked to a waiting microphone in front of the room and turned it on. Smoothing his tie and looking supremely confident, Dickie began to speak in clear tones.

"I've wanted to thank all of you for your service to our country for some time now. You are exemplary workers in extraordinary circumstances and...far from home. There's been an ocean and a war between us and our beloved nation for far too long. Now that the war has ended, I'm sure I'll be losing some of you as well. So today, of all days, I wanted to thank you while I still had the chance."

When he paused, a wave of thunderous applause swept the room lingering for several minutes. He glanced to the back of the room before holding up his hands for quiet.

"You've probably noticed General Morse and General Davis with us today as well as our military protection guard who have been with us night and day. Thank you, sirs, for your presence here today for what I'm about to announce."

Phyllis and Lorraine exchanged curious glances. What was Dickie up to?

He cleared his throat. "You know how I came into this position of Military Attache at the American Embassy in London. It wasn't by choice or by aspiration on my part. The selection by President Roosevelt was as surprising to me as it probably was to all of you. What made my selection even more difficult was the fact that I was replacing a man who was irreplaceable. I know that and you know that." Dickie smiled briefly before continuing.

"So that brings me to what we're here for today: to restore honor to an honorable man and exemplary praise for a job well done." He straightened to military correctness. "Please stand at attention for Lt. Col. Ronald Lawrence."

Out of the corner of Phyllis' eye, she watched their Ronnie slowly walk down the center aisle shaking hands as he went. Army officers stood at attention with crisp salutes but the civilians broke into applause, light at first, then building into a crescendo of sound. By the time Lawrence met Dickie at the microphone, there wasn't a dry eye in the place and hands were sore from clapping so vigorously.

Lorraine spoke into Phyllis' ear to be heard. "Ask him how the food is in the brig."

"Shh…"

Phyllis marveled at the impeccably dressed Army officer standing before the raucous crowd. It was several minutes before everyone quieted down and were persuaded finally to have a seat. Dickie stepped back, giving full attention to Lt. Col. Lawrence. Ronnie took a minute to compose himself, before lifting his head high to meet curious stares, happy faces.

"Thank you for coming today. I understand from Major Simpson that I have you all to thank for your continuing loyalty and belief in my innocence. I have nothing to say about the crimes committed against our country because those persons involved are being dealt with swiftly and efficiently. They will come before a military court of inquest within the week."

Light applause broke out and he lifted a hand for silence.

"I do, however, have something to say to certain persons who assisted in the investigation. Besides military police, members of the Federal Bureau of Investigation and MI5, I want to thank those present for going above and beyond their duties at the Embassy to prove I was innocent of all charges. I'm not going to name them here, but you know who you are and I'll be speaking with you privately." Ronnie smiled, looked around the room and settled his steely gaze on Phyllis and Lorraine making them sit up straighter. "You can count on that," he said looking right at them.

Phyllis gulped and didn't dare dart a glance at Lorraine. Her eyes slid from Ronnie's to an attractive man standing on a balcony, clasping the railing. Joe! Ronnie had mentioned MI5. Had Joe told him about her involvement? How much did he know anyway? Her eyes narrowed at him causing his grin to stretch across his face. Then he turned and vanished in the crowd.

Lt. Col. Lawrence thanked everyone for coming—more thunderous applause. He and Dickie left by a side exit with Embassy employees finishing their coffee and getting up to leave.

"That was unbelievable, Phyl! Ronnie! He's back!"

Phyllis laughed, picked up her purse. "I don't think he's back as Military Attache, but I'm sure he'll be posted somewhere. He's too valuable an officer to lose."

"I hope he doesn't retire after this whole episode."

"I don't think he will, but..." she shrugged, "I guess we'll see."

Phyllis and Lorraine filed out talking with their friends who were heading back to offices everywhere in the Embassy. At the staircase, Phyllis smiled at Lorraine before ascending to her office on the second floor. She couldn't see Joe Schneider anywhere, but that sure didn't mean the guy wasn't around somewhere. He had this sneaky habit of being everywhere she looked. Or maybe, she grinned, he was there because she was looking for him.

Phyllis opened the door to the Military Attache's office and turned on her typewriter. Just as she was reaching into her inbox to see what new correspondence Dickie had put in for her, the intercom buzzed. So he was in...

"Miss Bowden?"

"Yes, sir?"

"Would you come in my office, please?"

"Yes, sir."

Phyllis smoothed her curly hair, picked up her steno pad and pencil and opened the door to Dickie's inner office. To her complete surprise, Lt. Col. Ronald Lawrence was standing alongside Dickie.

"Hello, Phyllis." Ronnie gifted her with one of his breathtaking smiles.

"Hello, sir. How are you, if I may ask?"

"Fine, thanks to you, I understand." Lawrence strode quickly around the massive desk to engulf Phyllis in a tight hug. He straightened immediately but his smile remained. "I don't know the protocol in Army regulations to thank someone for saving his career, so a hug will have to do."

"Sir…" Phyllis paled. Dickie tried in vain to bite back a grin.

"No, allow me to finish. I want to thank you personally, as does my wife, but she's already back in the States with our daughters. I know you and Lorraine helped clear up this whole sordid mess and pin the blame on those responsible." He did smile then. "I once told Amy that you were clever and I'm so happy to have been right." He motioned for her to sit and perched on the edge of the desk.

"At ease, Bowden," he teased.

"Y-yes, sir."

"You found that note I put in your purse, I assume." When she nodded, he continued. "I'm sorry that I put you in such a dangerous position, but I was hoping it would steer you to the proper conclusions. I believe it did and that's the reason I'm standing here today. So thank you, Phyllis Bowden, thank you for your service and your belief in me." He crossed his hands over his heart. "Major Simpson was in a jam and you served him impressively." Dickie smiled and sat down behind him.

She reached into a skirt pocket, took out two small slips of paper and handed them to Ronnie.

"What's this?"

"Things I should have burned but never got around to it."

He looked the papers over and glanced back at Phyllis.

"I gave you one note. There's two here." He lifted the papers before handing them to Dickie.

She cleared her throat. "Right. I found the second in Silas Reardon's pocket." He arched an eyebrow. "I guess I have some explaining to do."

Ronnie smiled. "Maybe later."

192

"Sir. May I say something?"

"Please do."

"You took a big chance on me, Col. Lawrence. It could have all ended so badly."

"But it didn't and because of that, I want to ask you for a favor."

Her eyes widened. "Me?"

He nodded. "Yes, you. I've been assigned to the American Embassy in Oslo, Norway, and I would consider it an honor if you would come with me as my secretary."

Her jaw dropped. "Um..."

"Major Simpson has said he would hate to lose you, but will give you an excellent letter of recommendation for a job well done here in London." He tilted his head to one side. "So what do you say, Miss Bowden?"

Phyllis' smile lit up the room. "I'd love to go to Oslo with you, sir."

"I know you're on contract so you can finish the remaining time in Norway. You'd be the first American civilian in that country since its occupation by the Germans. They've fled and I can promise that Americans will be very popular when they start arriving."

"Sounds good, sir. When do we leave?"

"In two weeks. Is that enough time to get your affairs here in order?"

She nodded. "I believe so."

Phyllis and Ronnie looked at each other in mutual admiration for a moment before he straightened and reached out to her. She stood and shook his hand trying not to burst into tears. That wouldn't be secretary-like and she didn't want him to think she was a weeper.

"I'll be in touch, Phyllis. Take care."

"Thank you, sir."

Phyllis smiled at Dickie and turned to leave. "Oh, and there's a new letter in your inbox from me, Miss Bowden," said Dickie. "Try to get it to me before closing time today."

She gave him a mock salute before closing the door between their offices. She was so excited it was hard not to kick up her heels in glee! Norway! A new adventure, a new country and a new job! It was too much…first the Allies win the war with Germany and her career goes into overdrive. Phyllis plopped into her chair and took a good look around her. This was her job, her life and she loved it more than she could say.

Slipping paper into her typewriter, her thoughts strayed to handsome Joe Schneider and she wondered what he would have to say about her good news. She didn't have to wait very long to find out what he thought.

* * *

CHAPTER 41

"Do you mind that I'm going to Norway? It's far away from London and we won't be able to see each other as often." Phyllis moved her chair closer to Joe's as he reached out to clasp her hand.

"Of course, I mind." He kissed her hand softly. "But I'd never get in the way of such a fabulous career opportunity for you. We can write each other and phone."

"And visit," she added. "Don't forget visiting."

"Sure. I can get time away and hopefully you can too. Since you helped clean up Lawrence's good name, I bet he'll give you a blank check."

"Probably but I would never abuse his trust. My work is important to me."

Joe kissed her hand again and she leaned in to kiss his lips when burly Mick sidled up to their table. Angel's was crowded tonight with a guy playing a harmonica in one corner. Screeching from the harmonica threatened to drown out the noisy chatter.

"You can't hide back here, Miss Phyllis. I can see you and this here State Department fella too."

"Hi Mick." She smiled at him and held up two fingers. "God save the King."

Two beefy fingers joined her salute. "God save the King. You ready for another round? We got whiskey tonight and old John's cookin' Toad in the Hole."

"Of course, he is," kidded Joe.

"With sausage?" Phyllis asked sweetly keeping her eyes pinned on Mick.

He hemmed and hawed some before responding. "Well, no, Miss Phyllis. We ain't got no sausage, but old John makes it so good..."

"...You could swear you were eating sausage," Phyllis finished for him.

His smile beamed showcasing that missing front tooth. "That's right! But then you've eaten here every week for the past year. Since you've been such a loyal customer, I'll make sure old John does a crackerjack job for ya."

"Thanks, Mick."

When he brought out the whiskies, Mick stopped suddenly. "Embassy guy at the bar says you're leaving, Miss Phyllis. Say it ain't true."

"It is true, Mick. I've been assigned to Oslo, Norway."

"Well, if you're back to visit Joe here, make sure you stop in to see old Mick too."

"I will." She nodded. "I promise."

He turned to go but looked back. "You hear about Malcolm?" When she looked at him blankly, he shrugged. "Seems he's been arrested for war...what do ya call it when you make money off the war and you shouldn't?"

"War profiteering?" Joe supplied.

"Yeah," Mick pointed at Joe. "That's it. Thanks. Malcolm at the Blue Anchor was arrested for war profiteerin'."

"No kidding," said Phyllis innocently.

"Never saw that comin' but then he never seemed like a good egg to me, no how. Heard he watered down his whiskey." He smiled. "I'll bring out your food soon."

"Thanks, Mick."

Joe leaned over to whisper in her ear. "Your exploits aren't well-known yet."

"And we need to keep it that way."

"Maybe you could apply for a position with MI5. You'd look really cute in a stylish fedora and trench coat."

She kissed his nose. "I'm an American, remember? I'm sure they only want Brits for those jobs. Besides, I'm going to Norway!"

"Do me a favor, honey."

"What's that?"

"Promise me you won't fall for any cute Norwegians."

She giggled, lightly butted his head. "It might be tough, but I'll give it a try."

* * *

CHAPTER 42

The girls at Seven Addison Bridge Place gave a surprise farewell party for Phyllis the next weekend. It was a real surprise too; for once, she hadn't an inkling what they were up to. Lorraine had arranged for Joe to keep her away for a few hours while they put up posters and streamers all over the row house. Norma bought party hats from a store downtown and Mildred and Doris baked a sheet cake. Unfortunately, since they'd never baked a cake before, it collapsed slightly in the middle and resembled the humps of a really small camel. But no matter! Doris stuck her finger in for a taste and proclaimed it edible.

Lorraine had invited everyone at the Embassy and Norma invited people who knew Phyllis from the Red Cross. Soon the house was buzzing with excitement as others joined them, some surprised she hadn't already left. But a party was a party!

Mrs. Stewart was watching through the window for Joe and Phyllis' arrival. When she tiptoed away from the front door with her finger to her lips, everyone ducked behind furniture or hid in other rooms. Nearly thirty GIs and boys from Ipswich had come down for the fun and were currently hiding under tables and around corners. Lorraine was trying to keep them all quiet—quite a task—and there was much snickering and giggling in the still of the evening. And then breaking the silence, they heard…

"So you're visiting your dad first?" Joe's voice rang out strong.

"That's right, I…"

"SURPRISE!"

Phyllis' head twisted around and she jumped back, right into Joe's arms. He grinned and pushed her forward. "Go on, Phyllis. They're here for you."

Lots of voices filled the air with laughing and talking and people coming up to tell her congratulations. The girls had wangled several bottles of champagne somehow and the fliers had brought a bottle of Canadian whiskey. Mrs. Stewart even hung around for a while sampling the cake and a touch of whiskey. Just a touch...

Sparky told the girls that this party was as noisy as the one at Hyde Park a few days ago. Everyone seemed to have an opinion about what to do now that the war in Europe was over and what would happen with the war in the Pacific. A few stragglers wandered into the tiny backyard and Mrs. Stewart tried to corral them back inside so as not to disturb the neighbors.

With whiskey flowing, the cake and snacks being snapped up and happy people socializing, the party went on until the wee hours of the morning. Mrs. Stewart had long been in bed when the final folks left about three. No one cared if they had to get up early for work or had a presenting engagement they just couldn't miss. It was another celebration and the city was alive with them. After everyone had left, Phyllis and Lorraine brought dirty dishes into the kitchen to stack for washing, while Joe picked up cups and glasses left all over the house.

"Let's leave it for later," yawned Lorraine. "I'm bushed." She reached over to hug Phyllis tightly. "I never thanked you for rescuing me."

Phyllis smiled against her friend's moist cheek. "You're welcome. I know you would have done the same for me."

"What'd I miss?" The girls broke apart to glance at Joe standing a few feet away with a trash container filled with party hats and soiled napkins. Phyllis smiled at him. "Just a little girlfriend bonding."

"Oh." He grinned, set down the wastebasket and reached into his jacket pocket. "I forgot this letter earlier but Mrs. Stewart asked me to give this to you. You were busy being the celebrity of the moment with worshippers at your feet."

"Very funny, Mr. Schneider." Lorraine yawned again. "I'm heading for bed. Tell me about it tomorrow, Phyl. My eyelids are closing."

"Night, Lorraine."

"Yeah, get some sleep."

Lorraine hugged Joe before leaving the kitchen. "I need to thank you too for rescuing the both of us. I don't even know what all happened, but I wouldn't be standing here if not for you and Phyllis. So thank you, Joe."

He hugged her back. "You're welcome, Lorraine. Take care of yourself."

"Hey," said Phyllis. "You makin' time with my guy?"

The serious mood lightened and Lorraine went off to bed. Joe handed a long envelope to Phyllis. The return address made her eyes widen. She grabbed it, ripping it open quickly.

"Who's it from?"

"Amy Broadbent."

"Lawrence's secretary?"

She nodded with eyes focused on the page in her hand. After reading the letter through, Phyllis started at the top and read it again. A smile slowly bloomed on her tired face. Joe touched her cheek softly.

"Good news?"

"Very good." She stuffed the letter back into the envelope. "You knew that Amy tried to kill herself, didn't you?"

He rubbed his jaw. "I heard something about that."

"We had gone to party at the P51 Mustang base up in Ipswich and I heard the horrible news from the girls on the train home."

"…And thought you were somehow responsible?"

Her lips parted as she stared at him. "How did you know that?"

"Lucky guess…"

"Anyway, I saw her at the hospital and that's what spurred me into action."

"Amy's attempt at suicide pushed you?"

"Yes. I'm ashamed to admit I was floundering in denial until Amy jolted me out of my lethargy."

He clasped her hand in his. "Nicely put, but I'm not sure I'm happy about that. Although maybe I should be."

"Why?"

"Your nosing around got MI5 interested and that's one of the things that brought me into the case." He brushed his lips against hers and asked softly, "How is she?"

Phyllis smiled, held up the letter. "She's good. She wrote that Ronnie called her with the happy news that he'd been exonerated."

"What's she doing now?"

"Working for the Justice Department in Washington. She mentioned her new boss is a top flight attorney and she loves her job."

"Who's the new boss?"

"Maybe you've heard of him—Floyd Delavan."

"Oh, yes. Good guy."

"Too bad he's married. Amy says he's cute too, but very serious."

Chuckling, Phyllis walked Joe to the door. He held her in his arms for the longest time like he never wanted to let her go.

"By the way, did you call your sister? Mrs. Stewart asked me to…"

"Yes, yes, believe me, I got the message."

"And?"

"I called my sister, Mary Ellen, who told that Dad had rallied some with the fabulous news that the war was over in Germany."

"Did you tell her you'd be coming home? At least for a little while."

"I did."

Joe nuzzled her neck, kissed her softly.

"What's on tap for tomorrow? Want to do something? How about taking in some London attractions before you leave me?"

She touched his face. "I haven't left you yet and I'd love to see the sights with you, but I need to visit a friend first."

"A friend? Can't tell me who?"

"I'll tell you tomorrow night when we discuss our sightseeing plans for the day after."

He rolled his eyes. "Fine. Be mysterious. I'll call you tomorrow."

After kissing him goodnight, she turned off the lights and headed for her bedroom. He thinks she was being mysterious? Ha. She had nothing on Ann Fletcher, the original mystery woman.

Ann Fletcher.

She hadn't been as innocent as Phyllis first thought.

* * *

CHAPTER 43

The note taped to Ann's door was surprising. Peering in a window, Phyllis could see the flat was empty and deserted. In disbelief, she opened the note.

Phyllis,

I know what happened. Yes, a little bird told me what I wanted to know and another talky bird mentioned your involvement. I can only add how proud I am of you. You did good, dear, now go enjoy life while you're still young. Take care of yourself and I'll drop you a line when I'm resettled. Oh, I've returned home.

Love, Ann

P.S. Keep the hanky. I see you used it to good advantage and it's little more than a souvenir now, perhaps a souvenir of our time together. Be well.

Ann had returned to the States? Without telling her? Disappointment flooded her senses leaving her wistful and sad. She hadn't been able to say goodbye or tell her about her new posting in Norway. Phyllis had ridden the tube all the way over to Covent Gardens and walked several blocks to Ann Fletcher's little flat above a bookstore only to find Ann gone. Apparently for good.

She wandered listlessly back down the stairs to find a grinning Joe Schneider waiting for her at the doorway.

"It's disconcerting how you always know where I am."

"Just part of my job." He tilted his head to see her face. "Are you mad?"

"No." She shook her head slowly. "Sad mostly. Ann's gone."

"Was she a good friend?"

"The best."

He pointed to her hand. "What's that? Have you been crying?"

"No." She held up the hanky. "Ann gave it to me weeks ago after Ronnie was arrested. She was another little push I needed."

"Good grief." He pushed the hat back on his head. "Everyone tried to get you involved."

"Well," she sighed, "all's well that end's well." She stepped down to him and he wrapped his arm around her waist.

"Do we have to wait until tomorrow to see those sites you wanted to see one last time?"

She shook her head. "Nope. I have on my walking shoes, so let's have some fun."

* * *

CHAPTER 44

They wore out her walking shoes.

Joe and Phyllis visited Scotland Yard, St. James Palace, Big Ben, Ten Downing Street and Westminster Abbey. At Scotland Yard, she and Joe joked about the fact it was a building and not a yard at all. They went to Windsor to see the beautiful castle and on to Eton to watch small boys in their tall, silk hats.

Tea along the Thames was energizing before they walked back to Windsor and took a train to Slough. From there, Phyllis and Joe taxied to Stoke Poges, a small village north of Slough. Phyllis had wanted to visit the manor house where King Charles I was imprisoned in 1647 before his execution. The visit left her in a reflective mood, although Stoke Poges had been an inspiration to several English poets. She would soon be leaving a city and country she had come to love.

Back in London, Joe bought her a new hat at Harrod's and they had dinner at a Greek place on Regent Street. It was a comical sight to see the proprietor's family run madly around trying to help customers, but got in everyone's way instead. Lorraine joined them putting a funny ending to a wonderful day.

She stayed with Joe that last night in London, exhausted yet happy. And somewhat confused about leaving her English home first thing in the morning.

After tearful farewells to the residents at Seven Addison Bridge Place, Joe took her to the Air Transport Command terminal in plenty of time to catch a military transport to the United States. She was going home to visit her family on a week's leave in Virginia before needing to report to her new post in Oslo.

It was foggy when he walked her out to the plane. They turned toward one another and he buttoned one of her jacket buttons she'd failed to notice. After smoothing her collar and adjusting her hat, he finally looked into her pretty face.

"I was wondering if you were going to look at me." She tugged at a glove before reaching up to tip his fedora a little to the left.

"There. That's a more rakish angle for that hat." She straightened the lapels on his trench coat and glanced back at the C-47 transport plane revving up its engines behind them. Lights on the runway indicated the path Phyllis would soon be taking. She shivered, not from the cold, but from knowing that path would take her away from the man she loved. Phyllis cleared her throat; he needed to know.

Joe moved closer. "It isn't over between us, Phyllis Bowden. We'll figure this out."

"I know it."

He looked at the plane enshrouded with fog and back at her with a warm smile and twinkling eyes. "Here's looking at you, kid."

She laughed. "I look as much like Ingrid Bergman as you look like Humphrey Bogart."

"Maybe not, but the sentiment's right."

"You know I love you." She pressed her lips to his expecting a light peck. Instead, Joe curled a hand around her neck to hold her in place for a kiss that spoke volumes. Surety, confidence and a promise for the future were implied in their heart-stopping kiss. A door on the plane opened and they parted reluctantly.

"I love you too."

"And for now," she began.

"…That's all we need to know," he finished.

With a last loving look, Phyllis turned and walked to the airplane.

THE END

* * *

ABOUT THE AUTHOR

SJ Slagle lives in Nevada with her husband. They are both long time Nevadans mired in the Old West spirit. She has two grown sons and is interested in a great many topics, thus the necessity to write under two names: SJ Slagle and Jeanne Harrell.

From the Author

This book was an absolute pleasure to write. I would like to credit the diary of Milmae Floyd Gray, my cousin, for several events occurring while she lived in London in 1945. With family permission, I borrowed these events and fictionalized certain elements to enrich my historical novel. I wish to thank the family of Milmae Floyd Gray for their generosity in sharing her extraordinary life with me.

If you have any comments you'd like to share with me, please write me at **sindaslagle@gmail.com**. I would love to hear from you.

If you haven't signed up to received my newsletter, please do so. It will give you a catalog of my book titles and give you the latest information on upcoming books. **http://jeanneharrell.com/subscribe.html**

Would you please write a review? Wherever (book distributor) you purchased this book has a way to write a review. To thank you for doing so, please enjoy a chapter from **OSLO SPIES**, the next book in this series.

Norway is a destroyed country at the end of World War II. Enter Phyllis Bowden, a young woman in military intelligence, assigned to the American Embassy in Oslo after the Germans have retreated. Her already difficult job is complicated by the appearance of a runaway child and the disappearance of her fiancé, an Mi5 agent, putting Phyllis in the worst struggle of her young life and career.

* * *

"Don't be frightened."

The little girl looked from her terrified mother to her father, his face reddened from strain with purple veins bulging at the temple. She clung to her mother wrapped in the man's arms, all three locked in their teary embrace. Fear permeated the room with artillery exploding just outside. When the door flew off the hinges and the windows shattered with the next bomb, he pushed away from them both.

"I have to go. You know I have to go. I've stayed too long as it is. My company is loading on the fjord as I speak and if I'm captured...well, let's just say it won't be good."

"Oskar, you promised we could go with you."

"I can't take you, but if I can return some day, I promise I will."

That only made the mother and daughter cry harder. With the war exploding around them, a reunion didn't seem remotely possible. Death was more inevitable.

He scurried into another room returning with something in his hands.

"Take this, liebchen. You've been such a sweet girl and I'll miss you." Pressing his lips to her forehead, he placed the item in her arms before kissing her mother. His kisses were light, meaningful, but final. With that, the man brushed off his green uniform before rushing out the open door. She knew as well as her mother that if he'd looked back, they all would have been done for. It was crushing enough that their life together had fallen apart. And with the British forces invading the south and the Soviets coming in from the north, the girl knew her family would soon be no more. She wasn't sure why, but she knew it.

It had been in her father's lingering looks and the terror on her mother's face. Things were changing around her and these changes weren't going to be good. She looked down at the doll in her arms.

* * *

CHAPTER 1

Oslo was raw and exposed as if someone had sliced open the city's stomach and its contents had spilled out. Driving down a main street, blocks of tall, stout buildings would suddenly devolve into shattered husks of once thriving businesses. A square pile of bricks with the top floors blown away stared straight ahead unblinking with two glassless windows as eyes. Eyes as unbelieving as hers.

Devastation was everywhere, yet long lines of people queued by the open doorway of a soot-covered building that had miraculously survived.

It was a strange kind of nighttime—the kind with daylight instead of darkness. Being this close to the Arctic Circle, it should have been cold. But in July 1945, the weather was almost as warm as in Washington, DC where she'd just come from visiting her family.

Phyllis Bowden's lips stayed firmly closed and she wasn't going to ask, it wasn't her place. She held it in as long as she could, but the words escaped all too soon.

"Please, sir. What happened? I thought the German authorities resided in Oslo. It looks like the place was bombed."

"Ja." The word was pushed out of the Norwegian driver's mouth while he inhaled. "Volcomen Norge."

"Excuse me?" she asked.

"Welcome to Norway."

Not the welcome she expected. She'd just left her Embassy assignment in war-torn London to be assigned to war-torn Oslo. Both cities had bombs falling on them until the end of that horrendous war with Germany, but Phyllis had learned from classified reports that much of Norway's destruction was due to the Norwegian resistance that had wreaked the havoc she witnessed. Unlike other occupied countries, Norway had waged an internal war with the Germans like no other. She needed to know much more to be of any use here.

Phyllis glanced about the bus as it jerked clumsily along the debris-strewn street. The vehicle, along with many others, had been liberated from the Germans and was unlike any she'd seen. It was built with comfort in mind. Every cushioned seat had a table with a reading lamp and telephone. An impeccable lavatory filled with sweet-smelling soaps and soft towels was five feet away. Nubby carpeting covered the floor and the whole inside was spotless. Glancing out the window, beautiful blonde women with golden tans and white shorts rode by on bicycles. Many Norwegians she passed were wearing white and were dressed better than the English she'd just left behind. In London, there had been plenty of clothing to buy, but it was rationed. She wondered how the Norwegians could look so much better since there was not one article of clothing to be purchased in all of Norway.

The five-year German occupation had seen to that. She'd learned the Germans had stripped the country bare of anything of value. They'd closed most of the stores, halted the fishing industry and any exports. Children wore paper or fish scale shoes, wooden clogs if they could make them. Leather was an unheard of luxury. Even though the German occupation had ended, there was still little homegrown food, no clothing, rationed electrical power and no medicine. America and Sweden were sending supplies, she knew, but like starving people, Norwegians would have to limit their diet until stomachs were able to digest the vegetables, meats and

213

macaroni being donated. With an austere diet for five years, any fat in the new foods would make Norwegians sick.

Yet the glorious feeling of the people was a sight to behold, even at night queued in lines with happy smiles on their faces. She could guess the reason for their happiness: Germans were no longer in control.

"What's that?" she called out to the driver.

"A camp for German prisoners," he responded.

"Are they leaving soon?"

"Ja, we hope, but there's thousands who have lived here for years and it will take time."

Phyllis considered what he said until they passed a government building with a Norwegian flag, bright red with a blue cross, waving proudly from a flagpole nearby. Her gaze strayed to the crumpled Nazi flag near a trashcan before she noticed Norwegian policemen escorting a handful of young women. They wore similar dresses, like uniforms.

"Excuse me, driver."

"Yes, miss?"

"What's happening here?"

The driver slowed at a stop sign allowing Phyllis time to take a good look at the small crowd assembled. The young women were really young girls, not even teenagers.

"Those are Quisling girls," he told her in a gruff tone.

"Quisling?" She had read a classified report about Quisling, but wanted the driver's take on the situation.

"Ja. Vidkun Quisling." She heard him spit on the floor. "Scum who tried to take over Norway when Hitler," another spitting sound, "was in charge."

"He's Norwegian."

"And a traitor to his country."

"What will happen to him?"

"He's been arrested and I hope he's shot."

Phyllis was quiet watching the scene play out. One little girl, not eight years old, caught her eye as the driver pulled away. She glanced up to see Phyllis watching her and the fear on her small face was palpable. A policeman herded her with the other girls, but she ventured a brief smile to Phyllis before disappearing into the building.

"And these girls? What will happen to them?"

"Don't care, miss, but if they're shot, it's better than they deserve."

A thought nagged at her until they reached Army Headquarters. What could a seven year-old Norwegian girl have done that was considered so traitorous to her countrymen? She shook off the thought after arriving and being met by a State Department representative. He put her up for the night in an apartment with State Department personnel. There was a kernel of darkness in this newly liberated country. As much as she tried to overlook it, Phyllis knew this kernel would pop into trouble.

But hopefully not tomorrow.

* * *

CHAPTER 2

First thing in the morning, Phyllis got a call from the State Department man she'd met last night. Neither the Army nor the State Department was sure where to find a billet for Phyllis. She was a civilian working for the War Department and wasn't employed by any currently functioning entities. He told her she could stay a few more nights in State Department lodging which was fine. She had a nice apartment with a large living room, bath and bedroom with twin beds all to herself. But it was expensive to stay there, so she was anxious to find a more permanent place to live. Also her luggage hadn't arrived, but delays were as common as shortages and she thought no more about it.

Army Headquarters was in a building confiscated by retreating German officers. Phyllis rode the German bus to the mess hall for breakfast. Hasty introductions on the bus led to delightful conversations over bacon and eggs, toast and tea. Tea again. She missed coffee, but the PX had just opened and coffee wasn't available yet. After spending a year in England, she'd had plenty of tea and was ready to start her days with a strong cup of coffee once more.

They'd all commented on the dishes. Bold, black swastikas decorated each plate. One of the mess hall staff had seen her staring when her order was ready and mentioned the Nazi emblems would be scraped off soon. An involuntary shiver filled her with momentary dread. The swastika, the symbol of evil. She fought another shiver that threatened to make her appetite disappear, but she was hungry. Phyllis picked up her fork, cut into her eggs and began a new conversation with Jay, the woman sitting across the table. Before long, swastikas were forgotten and they made plans to see Oslo together that day.

Jay Lawlor and Phyllis both had a day off before a new workweek started, so they took off to see what they could see. They had met in London when Phyllis was working for the American Embassy and Jay was a diplomat with the British government. Now Jay worked in Oslo for the British Embassy and they were surprised yet thrilled to meet again. The world really was a small place, especially after the devastating war in Europe.

Gasoline and electricity were rationed, but a few trolleys were operating again. An ancient trolley with as much rust as paint lumbered to a stop on a public street outside Army Headquarters. Creaking brakes indicated a mechanical problem, but it didn't deter the riders within. Phyllis and Jay hopped aboard the vehicle packed with ordinary Norwegians going to work. It was standing room only. Phyllis stood next to a seated woman whose plain brown jacket showed evidence of having been repaired many times. Men wore hats shiny with age and all shoes were in disrepair, needing to be replaced. A few people with crossed legs exposed stiff paper stuffed into shoes when the soles had worn out. With the curious glances her way, Phyllis knew her relatively new clothes made her stand out as a foreigner. She was glad when downtown Oslo came into sight and she and Jay got off the trolley. Once it had squeaked away, Jay touched Phyllis' arm.

"Did you see the stares we got?"

"Yes," said Phyllis. "It gave me the willies." She pushed back her curly brown hair while looking down at her corduroy jumper and white buckskin sandals. "Didn't think I'd be overdressed today, but I guess I am."

Jay nodded. "I never stood out much as a redhead in London and Scotland, but I must look like an alien here."

Phyllis laughed. "But a pretty alien so I think we're safe enough." She nodded towards the street. "Let's get going. We're burning daylight."

They began walking down a street filled with people hurrying in different directions. A mass of cables crisscrossed overhead with lights hanging down every hundred yards or so. Broken bricks in the street and sidewalk made for treacherous walking.

"Be careful not to muss those saddle shoes. Get those at Harrod's?"

"I did," said Jay, "and it sure looked like a couple of those women on the trolley were ready to rip them off my feet."

The three-story buildings they passed were covered in grime. The occupation hadn't been hard on only the Norwegian people; every vehicle, every bicycle, every building, even the few dogs they saw looked exhausted. Everything needed a thorough wash, a fresh coat of paint, and a good meal. But the people couldn't have been friendlier. Everyone Phyllis and Jay passed smiled at them. Ladies nodded while gentlemen tipped their hats. Halfway into the block, they stopped at a small café for lunch. With a hastily repaired door and tape across cracks in the windows, the café had obviously just reopened. The shy proprietor met them at the doorway and escorted them to a corner table.

"God dag, mine damer. Jeg heter Arne." The timid man with threadbare clothes and frizzy gray hair handed them a thick piece of paper, an unreadable menu. He smiled hopefully, pushing the paper closer. Phyllis and Jay exchanged embarrassed looks.

"How much Norwegian do you know?" Phyllis handed the menu to Jay. "I just got here. You've been here a few weeks. Have a go at it."

Jay shook her head. "I know how to say good morning and where's the bathroom."

Phyllis laughed. "That may not get us any food."

"Well, I can point," added Jay, "but there's no guaranteeing what we'll get."

"Not a linguist?"

"Not even a little."

The man's smile widened. "Engelsk? American?"

They understood that and nodded.

"Ah!" He held up a finger and hurried into the kitchen.

"This isn't like Mick's place back in London, is it?" Phyllis glanced around the bleak interior with few tables and chairs. No one else was in the place. It hadn't been bombed, but showed signs of long disuse with barren walls and few foodstuffs on shelves. The forlorn atmosphere was just this side of desperate.

"No," Jay agreed, "but he's probably happy to be open again. I'm sure there was nothing to sell during the occupation."

Footsteps from the kitchen had Phyllis and Jay turning their heads to see the proprietor propelling a reluctant young boy towards them. His blonde hair stuck up in several places and his shorts were ragged. The frown on his face indicated he wasn't happy to be there.

"Engelsk!" The man proudly pointed to the boy. "Sonn." He placed his hand on his chest.

Phyllis smiled. "Your son?" She extended her hand to the boy. "Nice to meet you."

The man nudged the boy forward to clasp Phyllis' hand.

"Nice...to...meet du," he said hesitantly. "My name...Lars."

"Nice to meet you, Lars. I'm Phyllis."

219

"Fill...us," said the boy and the man together, looks of wonder on their faces.

She turned to Jay. "This is Jay."

Jay stretched out her hand to the boy who took it and repeated, "Ja-ay." He beamed triumphantly. "Nice to meet...du."

"Same to you, mate." Jay handed the menu to the boy with raised shoulders. "Food?"

His confused expression made Phyllis wonder if they'd ever get anything to eat. Suddenly, a smile spread across his face and he pointed to an item on the menu. "Farikal...iz...good."

Both Arne and Lars looked so proud that Phyllis and Jay could only smile and nod in return. The man and boy rushed back to the kitchen.

"What did we just order?" asked Phyllis.

"Wait a minute. I think I have a Norwegian language dictionary with me." Jay dug around in her purse and pulled out a small book. She thumbed through a few pages. "Here it is. Farikal: mutton stew."

"Mutton stew? Great." Phyllis spread her paper napkin on her lap and looked toward the kitchen. "Wonder what else is in it."

Jay smiled. "Guess we'll find out soon enough."

Just then the man, with a hastily donned apron, brought out two steaming cups to place before the women. He smiled and left quickly.

Phyllis glanced into the cup, held it up to her nose.

"What is it?" Jay eyed her cup suspiciously.

"Well, it's brown, so I think it's supposed to be coffee."

"Try it and see."

Phyllis snorted. "Want me to be the guinea pig?"

"Yes, ma'am."

She raised the cup to her lips and blew in it before taking a cautious sip. Phyllis swirled it in her mouth. After she swallowed, she glanced over at her friend.

"Well?"

"It's not coffee, but it's hot."

"Just what we needed on a summer day." Jay picked up her cup for a taste. "Not bad, whatever it is."

Phyllis' face scrunched in thought. "In my preparation for this assignment, I remember something about there being no coffee at all in Norway because they weren't allowed to import anything. I think this may be roasted rye."

Jay licked her lips. "It tastes nutty. I bet you're right."

"When in Rome," began Phyllis as she took another sip.

"…Do as the Romans do," finished Jay.

They clinked their cups and downed more of the brown liquid.

Arne and Lars brought in two large bowls with towels protecting their hands.

"That looks hot," commented Phyllis.

"Ja," said Lars. "Hot."

After placing the bowls on the table, they stepped back and watched anxiously as Phyllis and Jay picked up their spoons. Phyllis poked around in her bowl.

"Mutton, potatoes and cabbage." She blew softly on a heaping spoonful before putting it in her mouth. Her eyes widened. "Good!"

Jay dug in and they ate happily with Arne and Lars applauding briefly before hurrying back to the safety of the kitchen. Lunch went smoothly and Jay put some bills on the table when Arne brought the check. Phyllis glanced at the unfamiliar currency.

"Glad you got some Norwegian money. I'm new in town and haven't changed my money yet."

"Well, good luck when you try. With our diplomatic connections, we're able to get small amounts of kroner, but money is one of the big problems in Norway right now. They've got to stabilize the currency to get their economy back on track. If our embassies can't get kroner, we'd have to resort to the black market."

"Black market's big here?"

"Right now, yes, because there's little available to eat or buy, but it'll fade as soon as the supplies coming in lessen the demand. Good thing too," she said finishing the last of her rye coffee. "It's expensive to buy anything on the black market."

"I bet. Let's see more of Oslo."

A left turn out of the café and a few empty stores down took Phyllis and Jay right back to the war. They stopped abruptly with dropped jaws when remembrance of war time horrors stood in front of them.

The crass writing in thick white letters was slopped on the front of a store window. Phyllis didn't need to know Norwegian to understand what the words meant.

"Jode. Stengt." She took a steady breath. "I know Jode means Jew and I bet the next word means closed."

Jay dug out her dictionary, skimmed a few pages and nodded. "You're right." Shaken, she let the small book fall from her hand onto the dirty sidewalk. Her pale face reddened with anger. "Just when you think it's over, the hateful past sends you a reminder."

Phyllis leaned over to pick up the dictionary and hand it back to Jay. "We'll never be free of this war and all the horrors that were committed. Never. We probably haven't learned a tenth of what happened." She clenched her teeth so tightly that her jaw hurt. A calming breath slowed her rapidly beating pulse, but what she'd seen would never leave her memory. Of that, she was certain.

The store had once sold toys. A plastic horse and a small tea set with cups, saucers and a teapot painted in bright pink and blue sat in the dusty window. Phyllis looked past the display to broken toys scattered on the floor with shelves torn from the walls. An overturned desk sat in a corner with papers, headless dolls and ripped stuffed toys tossed about as remnants of another battle. The winners of the fight had caused absolute destruction of this tiny piece of Norway and had gone off to fight other battles. Tears pooled in Phyllis' eyes when she turned to see the moisture collecting in Jay's. Seeking understanding, Phyllis and Jay stood frozen even as tears slid down their faces. Finally, Phyllis wiped her eyes and reached out to hug her friend. They stayed that way until the noise of the street reached their ears shaking them out of their painful reverie.

"I can't even imagine. Can you?" asked Jay.

Phyllis shook her head. "Let's…concentrate on what we're in Oslo to do."

"And what's that?"

"To help put the country back together."

Small smiles eventually claimed their faces.

"I can do that," said Jay. "Let's go."

Another block down, they came to a city park. Instead of the usual grassy areas with trees and bushes, a small pond perhaps and children's play equipment, the entire park was covered with various plots of land with people working the land, growing gardens. It was a busy place with people hoeing, pulling weeds and harvesting. They walked over to the nearest garden for a closer look. An older man and woman were digging in the dirt. They continued their harvest and smiled benignly when Phyllis and Jay walked up, hands raised in hello.

"Potatoes." Phyllis watched the man with tattered pants and rope for a belt pull the hardy vegetable from the ground. His confident smile showed a broken tooth in front when he proudly held the potato up for his wife to see.

She had crouched down, working on another row and tugged free two heads of cabbage. They said something in rapid-fire Norwegian to one another before showing the vegetables like trophies to the women watching them. Jay sighed and laid her hand on Phyllis' arm as they moved away.

"My boss at the embassy told me to leave my money at home."

"Why's that?" asked Phyllis.

They walked down the many rows of gardens watching Norwegians doggedly pull, tug and cut the food from the ground. Potatoes, cabbage and carrots filled the baskets that lay scattered everywhere. People had the proud looks of mothers and fathers with newborn babies.

"Because," Jay sighed again, "he knew I'd want to give all my money away to everyone I meet."

The corners of Phyllis' mouth curved. "So you're a big softie."

"I am."

"Just think about all the good work you're doing at the embassy."

Just past the park, Phyllis and Jay came upon a building with an open front and Norwegian flags planted on either side. A small crowd of children was assembled, laughing and chattering noisily. Women in white paper hats lined up behind a counter to hand out bread and sausage to anyone who walked up. The children waved Norwegian flags and munched happily as they clustered around the sides of the building.

"What's happening here. I mean, I can see they're eating, but where did all this food come from?" Phyllis tapped the shoulder of one little boy. He was five or six years old wearing a slick rain hat. His rosy cheeks were stuffed with the bread he was eating and his eyes were bright with excitement.

"Ja? Hva vil du?"

She pointed to the bread. "Do you speak English?"

"Engelsk?" he asked.

"Yes."

"No." He shook his head and went back to eating his bread.

A little girl with blonde braids slipped alongside Phyllis and took her hand.

"I speak Engelsk. Du want food?" She held up a bun for Phyllis to take. Her angelic face nearly took Phyllis' breath away.

"No. Where did you get bread and sausage?"

She pointed to the building and the ladies. "They give us."

"But where…" The little girl dashed away to run up the street with another girl. Phyllis chuckled at the sight of twin braids flapping as she went. "Guess that's all I'm getting from her."

"May I help you?" One of the women distributing the food came around the corner. She wore an apron and looked as thin as all the other women Phyllis had seen so far in Oslo. With a limited diet for five years, no Norwegian looked fat or even sturdy. "I speak English."

"Great!" Phyllis swept a hand toward the crowd of children. "Where did all this food come from?"

The woman ran her hands down her apron and straightened her hat. She nodded at Phyllis and Jay before replying. "The bread and sausage were confiscated from German military stores. We hand them free to anyone who wants them. The children come day and night."

225

"No bread or sausage when the Germans were here?" asked Jay.

"We were lucky to have anything to eat. The first years of the occupation, grain, coffee and sugar were rationed. After that, we had nothing but the fish the Germans didn't want and whatever we could raise ourselves."

"Yes," added Phyllis. "We went by a park with gardens."

"Farmers did a little better than us in the cities, but not much. There was too much..." she seemed to be searching for the right word. "Spying."

"Spying?" asked Jay.

She nodded, glanced back at the other women. "Germans spying on us, traitors spying for the Germans." She blew out a shaky breath. "You didn't know who to trust." The woman thrust out her hand to Phyllis. "You're American, yes?"

"Yes, I am."

"Thank you for the supplies you are sending us."

She turned to Jay. "You're English?"

"Aye, mate." Jay's smiling eyes widened with surprise when the woman enveloped her in a fierce hug. Stepping back, she wiped away tears. They smiled broadly at one another.

"The English are our saviors. We can never thank you enough."

"It was our pleasure, ma'am."

With that, the woman returned to her job handing out bread and sausage to more children who had collected for their treats. And with heads held high, they continued their labor of love as Phyllis and Jay walked by smiling and nodding their approval. A tip of the head from Jay to the woman they had spoken to and they were gone from the pleasant scene.

CHAPTER 3

"Is that a fijord?"

"Yep."

"What exactly is a fijord?"

Phyllis opened Jay's dictionary, skimmed through and began reading aloud. "It's a deep, narrow lake drain with steep land on three sides. The opening toward the sea is called the mouth of the fijord and is often shallow."

Jay and Phyllis looked at the sight before them. Tall, snow-covered peaks surrounded the body of water with trails zigzagging through the trees to homes built in the mountains. Vivid blue seawater deepened in color farther away in the distance. Standing on a pier, Phyllis pointed to the beach below.

"Look! They're swimming."

Jay arched an eyebrow playfully. "Want to do it?"

Phyllis laughed and they headed down to the beach. Once at the water's edge, she stuck in a hand.

"You'd think it would be cold this close to the Arctic Circle."

"It's July," said Jay. She stuck in a hand as well to test the water temperature. "Warm..."

Glancing around the beach area, Phyllis spotted what she was looking for.

"There it is."

"What?"

"A guy renting bathing suits."

A tiny, wooden hut not far from the pier caught Jay's eye. As they walked towards it, many Norwegians in various kinds of clothing smiled and said hello. Some wore bathing suits, some were in shorts and long pants. A few women wore long, white skirts.

"Friendly people."

The man working in the hut wore a colorful sweater, shorts and a bright red knit cap. When the women walked up to him, a big smile creased his weathered face.

"Goddag, damer. Trenger en badedrakt?" When his request met with blank looks from Phyllis and Jay, he tried pointing at the row of bathing suits behind him. "Badedrakt?"

That, they understood.

"Two, please." Phyllis held up two fingers. The man discreetly checked out their figures, took two suits off the shelf and handed them over.

"How much?" asked Jay. When the man shook his head, she reached into her purse for the Norwegian dictionary. "Hvor mye?"

The man looked confused, probably due to her wretched Norwegian pronunciation, but pointed to a sign on the side of the hut.

"He wants five kroner per suit," Phyllis asked her. "How much is that?"

"About ten cents."

"Pay up, friend. I'll pay you back."

Jay shrugged, fished out her wallet. "Going on the town with you is getting expensive. I thought you Yanks had money."

"Some do and apparently, some don't. I promise to get cash tomorrow."

"I'm not worried." Jay smiled. "I know where you live."

They changed in a small restroom behind the hut and hurried down to the water. Stowing their clothes on a chair recently vacated,

Phyllis and Jay ran into the water, turned to one another to laugh before diving in. Phyllis was surprised and pleased at how warm it was. She swam underwater until she had to surface for a breath of air. What was it about water that seemed to protect and cleanse? Phyllis floated on her back for several minutes drinking in the impossibly blue sky overhead dotted with fluffy white clouds. It was a beautiful day and all seemed right with the world. Turning her head to the right and then the left, the mountains seemed larger from her new vantage point and she knew they'd been there for millions of years. They would stand for millions more.

The beauty of the area softened her sadness of what Norwegians had endured during the war. The cleansing water washed away thoughts of ruined stores and stolen goods, destroyed homes and stolen lives. But the water couldn't entirely wash away her thoughts about the children.

The children of Norway had perhaps lost the most: their hopes and dreams for the future, their abilities to laugh and play, to be children. Without that necessary developmental step, what would become of them?

Jay swam up behind and splashed water on her.

"Hey!"

"Well, you're thinking too hard and this is our day off. Think tomorrow."

Phyllis chuckled, paddled to a shallow spot where she could stand. "You're right. Tomorrow is soon enough for deep thinking."

"But I know what has put that serious look on your face."

"What?"

Jay's eyes swept the fjord and over to the beach covered with exuberant people talking and laughing. It should have been a typical scene in a typical beach town or port city. Her wet hair dripped from curly auburn strands onto her glistening cheeks and neck. "The beauty we see contrasts sharply with the terror we know was here for five years. It would be unbelievable if we didn't know it happened."

"I know what you mean. The reports I read of bombings, people shipped off to slave labor camps and other terrors make this moment incredibly poignant." Phyllis nodded toward the people swimming nearby. "I bet everyone here has a story to tell and is counting their blessings the Germans have gone."

Jay took a deep breath. "Come on. Enough philosophizing for one day. We need to get back."

After changing clothes and returning the bathing suits, the women hiked to the pier to catch a trolley back to Army Headquarters. Riding along in the rusted old vehicle with Norwegians going home after work, Phyllis looked thoughtfully around her. She was beginning to like Oslo and Norway very much, but when she turned to speak to Jay, something caught her eye.

Jay was babbling and pointing from her side of the trolley. "Can you believe it's still daylight? Blimey, it must be seven at night at least. Why, I could…"

"Jay." Phyllis tugged on her arm. "Look at that."

"What?" She glanced where Phyllis was looking. Her eyes narrowed just as her lips flattened to a tight line. "What is that?"

The bed of a large truck parked by the side of the street was filled with eight frightened women with shaved heads. Two women had black swastikas drawn on their foreheads and a paper sign with writing in Norwegian fluttered on a window.

"What the hell is that?" Jay and Phyllis stood immediately to get a better look out the window. "Why are their heads shaved?"

A woman next to them touched Jay's sleeve. "Samarbeidspartner." Another woman nodded in agreement.

"What?" asked Phyllis.

The woman was quiet a moment. "Quisling."

Jay thought that over. "They think these women collaborated with the Germans, like Vidkun Quisling. He was a Norwegian official who tried to take over the government when the king was deposed."

Phyllis' confused look became angry. She lowered her voice. "Yesterday when I arrived, policemen were herding young girls into a building. The driver called them Quisling girls."

"Sure," Jay whispered back. "I've heard of them. It was the Norwegian version of the League of German Girls, so-called youthful Hitler lovers. So?"

Eyes as chilly as her words met Jay's stare.

"Please tell me what a little Norwegian girl could have done to collaborate with Germans." She angled her head toward the women on the truck as the bus rolled past. "And please explain to me what shaving a woman's head is supposed to prove? What are they doing to men who collaborated? Are they shaving their heads too? Parking them out in trucks to be gawked and yelled at? This feels like stoning a woman for something she did in some barbaric third world country."

Jay spoke directly into Phyllis' ear. "This isn't your country or mine. We didn't live through five years of German occupation like they did. It's no telling how we would react had we been through similar circumstances."

"I understand what you're saying, Jay, but there's an unfair quality here, a dark wind blowing through this country. I'm not going to pretend to ignore certain things I see."

"Even if you understand why people are upset with collaborators?"

"Even then."

Jay tugged her away toward the front of the bus. "Let's go. This is our stop."

As they walked towards Army Headquarters, Phyllis ventured a last lingering look at the women on the truck. Something wasn't right; something felt off and she was determined to find out what it was. It could mean sticking her nose in where it didn't belong. Sometimes, she thought, a person just had to do that.

* * *

CHAPTER 4

Lt. Col. Ronald Lawrence, Military Attache.

Phyllis stared at the name painted on the frosted glass of the door. Standing on the second floor of the American Embassy in Oslo, Phyllis experienced a twinge of déjà vu. The name took her back to London where she'd been assigned as secretary to an officer. It took her breath away remembering that Lt. Col. Lawrence, Ronnie they called him, had been arrested for espionage and suffered needlessly until Phyllis and her friend Lorraine had found the proof of his innocence. Her pulse fluttered as names and places flashed through her mind: Dick Simpson, Wise Willie, Canning Town, Seven Addison Bridge Place and the dreaded Malcolm. It was enough to make her shudder and back away from the door when it creaked opened in front of her.

"Phyllis! It is you! I thought I heard a noise in the hallway. Come in. Come in! I'm glad you've finally arrived." Lawrence's momentary surprise softened to smiling eyes with a knowing look. He thrust out his hand.

"Sir. How are you?"

His energetic handshake left her in no doubt that he was glad to see her. He pushed open the door and swept a hand toward his office.

"Please come in. Let's get reacquainted."

Once she was seated in a chair by his desk, the tall man walked briskly around to address her. His smart brown jacket crinkled as he sat. His tie was expertly knotted and contrasted with his light brown shirt and pants. Straight military posture gave away his dedication to duty and service. Everything about Lt. Col. Ronald Lawrence screamed upstanding Army officer. But his intense look caused her to glance down at what she was wearing. Was her gray rayon dress too…dressy for the office? Maybe she should have worn a skirt her first day on the job or maybe…

"You're a sight for sore eyes, Miss Bowden."

"Colonel, we saw each other only two weeks ago in London."

"Yes, yes." He leaned forward in his chair. "How's the family in Washington? I heard your dad was doing better."

She nodded happily. "My sister was always sending me doomsday letters, but he's actually feeling pretty good."

"Cancer, is it?"

"Yes, but it's in remission. Since the war ended, he seems like a new man."

"I hope his treatments continue to go well."

"Thank you, sir."

"I know it's not my business to ask, but how is your young man, Joe Schneider. I believe he's an Mi5 chap."

She smiled. "And you would know that because you met him when he spoke to you about what Lorraine and I…our activities…"

"Yes, he told me some and Dickie told me the rest. It's something I'll never be able to thank you enough for doing, Phyllis. What you and your blonde friend did for me is beyond duty, beyond loyalty, beyond any thanks I can ever bestow upon you."

"Colonel, I…" Phyllis blushed. "That's too much praise. I did what needed to be done and luckily it turned out well." She met his intense stare with one of her own. "The whole scenario could have turned out very badly indeed."

"Indeed it could have, but it didn't." His eyes twinkled. "So how about I have Joe come for a visit very soon, if you want to see him." He snapped his fingers. "Red tape no more. How about sometime in the upcoming weeks?"

"You'd do that for us?"

"Absolutely." Ronnie sat back in his chair with folded hands on the desk. "I may have to stop praising you, but I can certainly throw in a perk or two for a job well done. How would that be?"

"Wonderful, sir."

His smile remained, although he grew serious. "Let's talk about the job now, shall we?"

"Yes, sir." Phyllis pulled out a notebook and pencil. "What will I be doing as your secretary?"

"The usual—letters, intelligence reports, supplies—but I need help setting up this office, Phyllis. It's a mess, which you couldn't possibly have noticed yet, and I need you to straighten up the system. For heaven's sake, the stationary is in German."

"German?"

"Sure. They were here for five years. Everything of value is in German. The telephone operators all speak German." He sighed audibly. "It'll take months to straighten things out just administratively."

"Filing?"

"Filing is the least of it. I want you running the office of Military Attache, working our communication lines with Washington, handling queries from Norwegians who come to the embassy for help…as well as…something else."

She looked up from jotting in her notebook. "And what's that?"

Lawrence stood, straightened his jacket and walked to the window. The view from his second floor office looked over parts of

Oslo, on out to the Oslo Fijord. She could see the breathtaking scenery from where she sat. After staring out the window for a moment, he walked over to close the door. Once he had returned to lean against the desk, his eyes and voice became somber.

"You've proven your abilities one hundred percent, Miss Bowden. I want to take you a little further into the organization."

"Sir, I've already had tradecraft training for my job."

"I know but this will be more intensive because I intend to send you out on assignment occasionally."

"Out of Norway?"

"No, but I need eyes and ears in the city and perhaps out in the countryside."

"Um…" She put her pencil down.

"No need to get worried, Phyllis. It wouldn't be anything you didn't do in London—parties at the embassy, state department, Army and Norwegian officials, some travel."

"Parties?"

"And meeting certain officials occasionally. I'll need you to glean different kinds of information than you gathered for us in London. I can tell you more as the time comes. You know," he offered, "as the need arises."

"All right, if that's what you need."

"You still look worried, Phyllis. What is it?"

"Sir, I don't want to carry a gun and I would prefer not to be involved in anything dangerous."

He laughed. "This from the woman who wrestled a killer for his revolver in the middle of a V2 bomb explosion."

"And got shot for my efforts."

"All the more reason for more training."

She tried not to roll her eyes. "I was doing what needed to be done, sir."

"Phyllis." He leaned over to touch her hand. "Not only did you save your friend's life, you saved mine."

Her cheeks warmed with his praise.

"You've been in military intelligence ever since you stepped off the transport plane in England, Miss Bowden. I'm just asking that you do the occasional assignment for me."

When she still looked unconvinced, he continued. "General Donovan will thank you personally."

"I've met him already, sir."

Lawrence watched her a minute before his eyes widened. "Sure, I remember. Didn't he fish you out of the Potomac River when the boat you were in broke down? That was way back before you transferred to England, wasn't it?"

"It was."

"It's good to have friends in high places."

They smiled knowingly at one another.

"Do you have any questions about Norway that I can answer?" He walked around the desk to sit down.

"Yes, I do. I went around Oslo yesterday, just to see the city, and wondered about some things I saw."

"Such as?"

"I saw terrified women in a truck with shaved heads and swastikas painted on their foreheads. What's that about?"

He shook his head wearily. Glints of silver in his dark hair seemed more pronounced. "The Norwegians are a fiercely proud people. The resistance here was stronger than I've ever seen in an occupied country. We're still learning of the heroic deeds done by ordinary citizens and even children to push back at the Germans." He glanced over. "You know who Vidkun Quisling is?"

"Yes."

"Well, his name has become synonymous with traitor. Anyone who collaborated with the Germans in any way would be labeled a quisling."

"The women I saw? What did they do?"

"It could be anything from merely cleaning a German officer's house all the way up the scale to sleeping with a German. What's happening now, Phyllis, is a national purge."

"A purge?"

"Purge, witch-hunt, they mean the same in this context. Anyone who had anything to do with the Germans is being purged from society. Right now the well-to-do Norwegians who socialized with Quisling are hiding in their homes hoping to be spared. But they won't be." He paused. "Maids, window-washers, barbers and even clerks who did the slightest thing to help the Germans are being jailed or loaded on trucks to take to slave labor mines."

Phyllis jaw dropped. "You're kidding."

He shook his head. "I wish I were. It's going to get worse before it gets better, so...watch your step."

"Why? I'm American."

"You'll be dealing with all sorts of problems that the Norwegians are having. President Truman has asked that we cooperate fully with the Norwegian government to help get the country going again. We'll need to be tactful in what we say and how we act."

Phyllis glanced out the window. Bright streaks of sunlight reflected on the floor and walls.

"I haven't gotten used to a new president yet, Colonel. I'm still grieving for President Roosevelt."

"I know how you feel. Donovan's tearing out his hair because Truman is making noises about dissolving the organization."

Her eyes widened with surprise. "Really? Dissolving the Office of Strategic Services? How would that affect us?"

"No idea. We'll all find out together, I fear."

Something else occurred to her.

"You mentioned children, sir."

"Yes, the schoolchildren antagonized the Germans something fierce. They'd sing the Norwegian national anthem when they weren't supposed to, and wore national clothing like red caps or paper clips on their jackets."

"Paper clips?"

Lawrence shrugged. "It has to do with sticking together. When you saw a paper clip, you knew that person was with you in resistance. Teachers and the clergy are especially sainted since so many of them refused to follow Quisling's orders on Nazi propaganda, and ended up in labor camps or concentration camps."

She was quiet a moment. The swirling blades of a fan made the only noise in the room. Lawrence brushed a fleck of lint from the sleeve of his jacket.

"Anything else you want to know?"

"When I arrived, I saw a group of young girls going into a building being escorted by Norwegian police. My driver said they were Quisling girls and he wouldn't care if they were shot."

He nodded knowingly. "The children were required to be in these Nazi organizations from age eight and older, boys in one and girls in another. It's similar to the Hitler Youth in Germany, a step-by-step indoctrination into becoming a Nazi."

"These were little girls under ten years old, Colonel."

A look of sympathy swept his face before disappearing. "I know it, but they've been tainted with the Quisling brush and the purge is blind right now. Anti-German feeling is overwhelming and pervasive." He pressed his lips tightly together. "You know we can't get involved in that kind of internal country politics, right?"

"They were just children."

"Children on the wrong side doesn't cut any mustard with Norwegians. Stand apart from this, Phyllis. I've got plenty for you to do without you getting into trouble by trying to 'do the right thing'." His fingers dipped to put the phrase in air quotes.

"The right thing for us…"

"Is not necessarily the right thing for a Norwegian."

"…Huh. I'll have to think about that, sir."

Lt. Col. Lawrence stood and Phyllis did likewise.

"That's all for now, Miss Bowden. Your office is right out the door. Get acquainted with your equipment and deal with whatever walks in the door."

"Is there a supply closet close?"

"Yes, and Dickie said you've had a few problems getting stuck in supply closets. Anything you care to tell me?"

"I…ah…I've had a slight fear of closed places, sir. But…I'm fine now."

His eyes narrowed. "Okay. Thanks for the information. I'll keep that in mind."

"Thank you, sir."

Settled at her new desk viewing the electric typewriter, phone and Dictaphone, Phyllis thought about what Ronnie had said. What's right for one person may not be right for someone else. Sure, but when it came to children? Why wouldn't everyone be on the same page? Especially in light of how Scandinavian countries feel about their children. She'd read reports that the well being of children was of the utmost importance in their culture.

Phyllis chewed on her pencil eraser gazing distractedly at the papers piled on her desk. She should get to work, but thoughts circled in her mind.

Children are impressionable and want to please. Whoever got to them first would make the impression. Does that make them bad? Does that make them bad forever? She supposed it would depend on the children's actions.

Agitated, she shook her head to shake loose the unwanted thoughts and picked up a piece of stationary to write a letter home. Her eyes read the phrase at top of the paper.

"Der Reichskommissar Fur Die Besetzten Norwegischen Gebiete." She looked around for a language dictionary and skimmed through to find the words needed for a translation.

"The Chief for the Occupied Country of Norway."

Oh boy. Wouldn't her family back in Washington and her friend Lorraine in London be surprised to receive a letter on German stationary? A few letters for souvenirs and then she would throw out the rest. Maybe she'd send Joe one too.

Time to get this office in shape.

* * *

CHAPTER 5

The noise in the mess hall bounced off the walls. All the American diplomats and military working in Oslo ate meals at the officers' mess in Army Headquarters. German buses picked up employees with the War Department, American and British Embassies, State Department and other military and government staff each day to deliver them to the mess hall. With several days under her belt now, Phyllis noticed the swastikas had been scraped off the plates and she smiled at the Army's efficiency.

"What are you smiling about?" Jay reached up to smooth her hair made frizzy from the morning rain. Phyllis watched her try to control her upswept hairdo.

"You know, I had a roommate in London with red hair and she never had the problems you have."

"Did her bloody hair dryer ever conk out leaving her knackered?"

"Crikey," said Phyllis. "Would you please speak English?"

"I have this big old clunker of a hair dryer that, of course, doesn't work well here."

"So how do you dry your hair?"

"I do exercises and stand in front of the fan in my living room."

Phyllis laughed. "Mine works a bit better…when I have electricity, which is only sometimes."

"True. So tell me what you're so happy about today."

Phyllis stabbed a fork into her spaghetti and twirled it neatly before popping it into her mouth. As soon as her lips closed around the fork, a happy sigh escaped.

"You're enjoying your food too much, missy." Jay pointed a finger at her. "You'll be gaining weight next."

"No chance. I run from morning to night in this job."

"What's up?" Jay cut a bite from her sliced ham before dipping it in mustard. "This mess has the best food."

"To answer your question," began Phyllis. "I was smiling at Army efficiency, but then it hit me why it's so efficient."

"And why is that?"

"People like me are working their butts off, to be frank. There isn't a lazy person in sight. Everyone has a job and by God, they're doing it to the very best of their ability." Phyllis twirled more noodles. "I've worked in the Pentagon and the embassy in London, but the Army operation here has them all beat."

"Who says Americans can't get things done?" Jay said with a smirk.

"No one I know."

"Which brings me to my preferred topic today."

Phyllis glanced over at her. Jay's peaches and cream English complexion had two patches of pink contrasting with her hair color. Jay was such a take-charge kind of gal…was she embarrassed about something?

"Preferred topic?"

"A friend of mine has a problem, Phyllis. I was wondering if you could help."

"Sure. What's up?"

She watched Jay turn her head slightly and beckon to a slim blonde woman, very young, who began walking over to their table.

"Please bear with me here," Jay muttered quickly. "She's Norwegian. I didn't know who else to ask."

Curious now, Phyllis smiled at the pretty woman joining them.

"Phyllis Bowden, this is Astrid Hansen. She works in the British Embassy with me as a clerk."

Phyllis held out her hand. "Nice to meet you, Astrid. Would you like to join us?"

"Yes, thank you, but just for a moment." Her sunny hair was swept back with two small combs leaving short curls to play on her neck. It was an attractive hairstyle making her look older than she probably was.

"Pardon me for asking, Astrid, but you don't look old enough to work at the embassy."

Astrid blushed deeply. "That's kind of you to say, miss."

"Please call me Phyllis."

In the pause that followed Phyllis glanced at Jay who was looking at Astrid. When no one spoke, Phyllis cleared her throat.

"Now that we're all here, tell me what's on your mind. I'm betting this wasn't a random encounter."

Jay nodded and then with much effort, Astrid began to speak. "I'm from Trondheim."

"Trondheim? Up north?"

"Yes, Miss Phyllis. My family has been there for generations."

When she paused and nervously played with the hem of her blouse, Jay leaned forward. "Phyllis is my friend, Astrid. She may not be the one who can help you, but she's a good place to start. Please continue."

Even more curious, Phyllis straightened in her seat, gave her full attention to the young woman with wary eyes flitting around the room. Finally, she focused on Phyllis.

Astrid bit her lip. "When the Nazis came a few years ago, they tore down our churches, took away our food and issued ration cards." She swallowed so hard Phyllis could see her throat muscles contract.

"Do you need some water?" She pushed her glass forward. Astrid grabbed it and took a quick gulp. Still clutching the glass, she began again.

"Our ration cards were stamped with the letter J." She watched Phyllis carefully. "Do you understand?"

Phyllis' eyes swept to Jay and back. "That means you're Jewish."

"Yes, miss."

"I'm hesitant to ask this, but since you opened the door…did your family members survive the war?"

"Several of my extended family, cousins, aunts and uncles, left for Sweden when we heard the Germans were coming. My family waited for my brothers to return from the university here…"

"In Oslo?"

"Yes, but as soon as they got back, the Nazis took them and we haven't seen them since."

"The rest of your family was all right?" Phyllis steeled herself for the worst. She wasn't disappointed.

"No. My father is a rabbi and he and my mother were detained before being deported on the Donau."

"The Donau?" Phyllis' eyes slid to Jay.

"It was a German cargo ship used as transport between Germany and Norway," replied Jay. She glanced at Astrid before continuing. "It was called the 'slave ship' because so many Norwegian Jews transported on it were sent to…"

"Auschwitz," finished Astrid. Her gaze was on the table where tears began to dot the tablecloth. Phyllis' eyes filled up in response.

"I'm so sorry, Astrid. Do you know what has become of them?"

"No. There's been no word." She looked up then, eyes filled with resolution as well as tears. "That's why I asked Jay to see if she could help me. She's had no luck, but thinks that you, as an American, might have different resources."

"To do what exactly?"

"Find out what happened to my parents. Find out what happened to my brothers. There's not a day that goes by, an hour, a minute that I'm not thinking of them and wondering." She swallowed again. "I have to know. Whether it's good news or bad, I have to know."

Phyllis processed her request watching and admiring the courage of the young woman. She wasn't sure if she would be able to stand upright if her entire family had disappeared without a trace.

"May I ask you a question?"

"Certainly," replied Astrid.

"Are you the remaining member of your family?"

"I have a sister four years younger."

"You obviously weren't picked up by the Germans, so how did you escape?"

Her blush returned deeper than before. Her eyes flitted to Jay who nodded.

"Is it a secret?"

"No, miss, but it could be dangerous for me if anyone found out."

Phyllis' eyes narrowed. "I promise I won't tell a soul."

Astrid's bitten lip began to bleed. She blotted it with a napkin. "A…German soldier was lodged with us."

"He lived with you?"

"That's what the Germans did all over Norway. There was no housing, so any Norwegian with a house had to put them up." She paused, glanced around the room. "First I must declare myself a true Norwegian and never did anything that was against my country."

"It's okay, Astrid," encouraged Jay. "Go on."

Astrid lowered her voice. "The soldier who stayed with us was not much older than me. Sometimes when my parents were gone, we would talk. I know," her jaw jutted out defensively, "we were supposed to ignore the soldiers and not give them any attention, but I was lonely too. The Nazis had closed the schools and churches and we couldn't gather with friends, if any were even left."

Phyllis nodded. "It's okay. Please continue."

"So we talked some. I know a little German from my grandparents. Anyway, he was…lonely, missed his home. He wasn't as mean as many of the other German soldiers in town. In fact, he was actually Austrian and had been a baker in Vienna. I thought maybe he didn't like being a soldier very much."

"He was conscripted to fight in the German army."

"So he said." She spoke to the folded hands in her lap. "One day he told me that he…liked me and wanted to help our family. When I asked him how he could do that, he whispered that my parents were probably being detained as we spoke and soldiers would be coming for me and my sister next."

Phyllis blinked. "What did you do?"

"He told us to take what food and clothing we could and pretend to be going to the forest to cut wood. He told us to…hide. There were others hiding in the forest he knew, but his commanding officer wasn't interested in finding them. So he told me to go. He even helped my sister and I pack a few things. For some reason, he was very nice to us."

"So you and your sister escaped."

"Yes, Miss Phyllis, but I am no quisling." She looked Phyllis in the eye. "All we ever did was talk a few times. Like I said, he was homesick and said I had a nice family."

"Even though you were Jewish."

"One time he said he knew many nice Jewish families in Austria, but kept his feelings to himself."

"That young man doesn't sound like a typical German soldier."

Astrid shrugged. "I don't know. All I know is that he looked the other way when my sister and I fled the house and didn't return. No one came looking for us in the forest."

"How did you survive?"

"We met other villagers hiding out and lived with them until the war's end. Eventually, townsfolk came to find us and we went back into town. That's when the British had raided," she paused to smile at Jay, "and the Russians had come in from the north."

"That must have been very scary for you and your sister."

"It was but we had each other and prayed every day to find our brothers and parents once again."

She sat back exhausted. A shaky hand picked up the glass and drank down the water. When she looked at Phyllis, the tears had dried and her face was set with determination. At that moment, so was Phyllis. She nodded once.

"I can't promise anything, but I'll see what I can do. Remember when all is said and done, I'm just a secretary."

Astrid smiled and rose. "Thank you, Miss Phyllis." She turned to Jay. "I'll see you back at the office."

When she'd gone, Phyllis pushed back her plate of spaghetti.

"Lost your appetite?"

"I'll say."

Phyllis' brows drew together over narrowed eyes. "Why the ambush, Jay? Did you think I'd say no?"

"I'm sorry about that."

"No, you're not."

"Let me finish. I am sorry to have sprung Astrid on you like that, but we both know you're more than a secretary to the Military Attache at the American Embassy here."

"Whatever are you talking about?"

"Please." Jay rolled her eyes. "I'm not dumb. I have tradecraft training too."

"Are you..."

"...We say nothing aloud and there's nothing overt, but I can recognize one of my own when I see her."

Phyllis leaned back in her chair, her gaze fixed on Jay's intent stare. "Was our meeting again some kind of set-up?"

"No." She shook her head. "No, it wasn't and no one has put me up to this, but I'd like to help Astrid. There are many people in her situation, having had loved ones up and disappear and hers isn't the last request you'll get while you're in Norway." She lowered her voice. "You have good resources, Phyllis, and can make discreet inquiries without raising eyebrows. All I'm asking for is a little assistance to help my clerk."

"I don't know."

"You saw the effort it took for her to tell you her story. She's devastated and is trying so hard to make a life for herself and her little sister."

"Does she want to go back to Trondheim?"

249

"No, there's nothing left. The Germans burned most of the town when they pulled out. Her house is gone and many of her neighbors have scattered. She knows there's nothing there for her."

Phyllis was quiet, composing her thoughts before speaking. She raked fingers through her curly brown hair like she was plowing a field. Her eyes caught Jay's.

"Every single day I learn something new, some new atrocity that happened to the Norwegians. Even though Germany wanted to annex Norway, they seemed intent on destroying it those last few years. It amazes me they thought different countries and people would just…go along with Hitler's big plan."

Jay waited. She pushed back her plate as well, leaving half her lunch to wait with her.

"I told Astrid I would see what I could do. I'll keep my word, but it may be too soon after the war to get that kind of information."

"All I ask is that you try."

"…All right. I can try."

"Thank you, Phyllis Bowden. I know you'll be successful."

Phyllis and Jay rose to take their trays to the garbage bins. Scraping food into one bin, Phyllis put her plate in another. "And how do you know I'll be successful?"

Jay grinned. "You forget I knew you in London. I know what you did to help Lt. Col. Lawrence when he was arrested for espionage."

"That wasn't common knowledge."

"It was to people in our line of work."

Phyllis shrugged. "Okay, have it your way. I'm not even going to ask what you meant by that."

"Don't."

They left on the German bus for their respective offices. When it stopped at the British Embassy, Jay nodded to Phyllis.

"Keep in touch."

"I have a sneaky boyfriend just like you, Jay Lawlor."

"Really? How so?"

"He always knew where I was somehow and I have a feeling you're going to be just like that."

Jay laughed and stood up. "Can't wait to meet him then. See you later."

When Phyllis returned to her office at the American Embassy, Ronnie was waiting for her. He buzzed her intercom.

"Come in here, would you please, Miss Bowden?"

"Yes, sir."

When she walked into Lawrence's office, Ronnie sat there with a big smile on his face and a long, white envelope in his hand.

"What's that?"

"It's for you."

"For me?"

He chuckled, extended the envelope to her. "Don't look so surprised. It's from Joe."

* * *

Available now with Amazon at:
https://www.amazon.com/SJ-Slagle/e/B00U33WYZI/ref=sr_ntt_srch_lnk_1?qid=1492903828&sr=8-1

Enjoy these books from SJ Slagle available on all major distributors in ebook and paperback. Some titles will soon be on audiobook.

Sherlock and Me Series
The Case of the Starry Night
The Case of the Feathered Snitch
The Case of the Ghost Horse

Single title
The Reunion
London Spies

Enjoy these books from Jeanne Harrell available on all major distributors in ebook, paperback and some selected titles are on audiobook.

Rancher Series
Rancher's Girl
Whisperer
Always and Forever
Being Emma
The Darkest Hour
Just Before Dawn
Rancher's Christmas

Westerners Series
Riding the River
Stream Ran Dry
Lonesome Creek
Cool Water

Avila Beach Winery Series
The Winemaker's Dilemma
Winemaker's Son

Single Titles
Persuaded

These Nevada Boys
Courting Polly's Daddy
Never Let Me Go
Shoulda Been a Rancher
Since I Fell for You

Coming soon!
Touch of Magic

# # #

Made in United States
Orlando, FL
06 March 2023

30736162R00152